Defying her Mafioso

TERRI ANNE BROWNING

USA Today Bestselling Author

TERRI ANNE BROWNING

Defying her Mafioso

The Vitucci Mafiosos
Book 1

ISBN-13: 978-1539343400
ISBN-10: 1539343405

Prologue

Scarlett

The aching that was pulsing throughout my entire body woke me. The first thing I realized was that I was in a bed that wasn't my own. The sharp, worn springs were digging into my back, making it ache that much more. I wasn't some delicate princess who couldn't sleep on a damn pea but, shit, those springs hurt. Slowly I lifted my eyes, but the dimness of the room didn't help determine where I was. I barely made out a chair beside the bed and a sink across the room.

A toilet would have been nice. I had to pee so fucking bad my bladder ached too.

The smells hit me before I could even get my eyes open. Damn decaying wood. Cigarette smoke that seemed to linger throughout the entire room and burned my sinuses. Worst of all was what smelled like ripe garbage that had been left in the sun for days. It was enough to turn my stomach.

I blinked, trying to adjust my eyes a little faster so I could see what else was around me—what kind of danger I was in. The blurring of my vision slowed the process down, the ache in my head and the nausea rolling in my stomach telling me I probably had a concussion. I couldn't feel the presence of another person, but given the amount of pain I was in, my senses could have easily been off.

Carefully I shifted my arms and moaned before I could call the noise back. Jesus Christ, that hurt. They ached the worst and I realized why almost immediately. They were tied above my head on the bed. There was no slack to let the blood flow freely through my limbs and the slight shifting of them had sent a shot of agonizing pain straight down my arms to my shoulders.

Ciro.

His name was like a balm to my mind if not my body. I wished he were there, but knew if he had been I wouldn't have been experiencing the pain I was currently in. The person who had stupidly taken me would be dead for even daring to think of doing the things that had been done to my body.

Tears stung my eyes as the full force of the pain my body was in hit me, but I forced them back. I bit into my bottom lip to keep any more whimpers or groans from escaping as I took stock of the rest of my body. I had to keep a clear head. It could be the difference between life and death.

My legs were tied to the other end of the bed but they didn't hurt nearly as bad as my arms. My chest was throbbing, especially on the right side, and as I sucked in a deeper breath I realized I probably had a broken rib or two. Lowering my head to the bed once more I tried to think through the fog caused by the concussion.

How had I ended up here?

The last thing I remembered was dancing at some club downtown with my sister. Victoria had needed a night out so we had gone out for drinks and to unwind with some dancing. I'd needed to go to the bathroom but she'd been so lost in her own misery that I'd left her at the bar before going alone.

I wasn't expecting to be gone for more than five minutes. I'd walked into the bathroom and then… Nothing. I didn't remember anything after that. Not even relieving myself.

Was Victoria okay? The thought had a new fear piercing my chest and anger burning through my veins.

Had they taken her as well? Was she in another room, hurt and afraid?

Just thinking about the possibility had my nausea threatening to overtake me and I nearly retched. I'd slaughter anyone who touched my sister.

I closed my eyes as I listened for signs of life outside the room I was in. Nothing. No creaking boards. No TV. No traffic. No birds chirping. If Victoria was there she wasn't making herself known. Where the hell was I? The lack of noise was almost deafening and for a moment I had the real fear that they had fucked my head up so bad that I'd lost my hearing.

Another moan left me and my heart lifted slightly in relief as the sound echoed off the walls.

Damn it. I had to stop that.

A new sound reached me. Scratching feet that sounded like they were in the walls. Mice? Rats? Opossums? Maybe a raccoon? Hell, I didn't know, and as long as they stayed in the walls I would be just fine. If I saw one though… Damn, I needed to pee so bad.

Ciro.

I swallowed back his name, knowing if I spoke it aloud then there would be no force in the world to keep my tears at bay. I wanted Ciro. Needed him more in this moment than I'd ever needed him before. I knew he would come. Ciro would save me.

And then he'd help me kill them all.

Ciro. I need you.

Chapter 1

two weeks earlier

Scarlett

Jetlag had officially set in. I didn't want to move, let alone get out of bed, but apparently my day had already been mapped out whether I liked it or not.

"Come on, sleepyhead. Let's have breakfast and then maybe we can talk Papa into letting us go shopping."

I lifted the pillow off my head to look up at my twin. She was my exact copy in appearance, but our personalities were so different it was like we hadn't even come from the same mother. Victoria was a morning person. She was actually fucking happy when she woke up—most mornings. She saw the beauty and the good in everything and everyone. Papa said she was so much like our late mother that it almost hurt.

I, however, was so much like Vito Vitucci there was no denying I was his daughter. It took a miracle—or my sister's persistence—to get me out of bed before noon, and I sure as hell wasn't happy when I opened my eyes each morning. I was moody—an all out bitch more often than not. I trusted maybe five people in the entire world, because I saw the darkness in everyone. A darkness that was in myself just as much as them.

"If I didn't love you, I'd shoot you in the face," I mumbled, only half joking.

Victoria giggled, a sound that rarely escaped me but I loved hearing from her. She was the light to my dark and I needed my twin to survive. "Come on, Scarlett. I'm bored out of my mind and I haven't eaten since that tiny little sandwich we had on the plane last night. If I don't eat soon I'm going to be sick."

She knew which buttons to push. My twin had to eat regularly because of her diabetes. The little minx was always using it to con me into doing things I didn't want to. "I'm up," I said with a huff. "But if you think I'm putting on clothes yet, you are out of your pretty little mind."

"I promise to buy you an espresso while we shop." She grasped my arm and started tugging, because even though I'd told her I was up, I was still lying there with my eyes threatening to close again. She was twenty-one years old, for fuck's sake. She could eat breakfast alone in her own home, damn it.

"But…sleep, Tor. I want sleep," I whined as she grasped my arm with both hands and used her little strength to pull me off the bed. As I reached the end, I just let gravity take hold and I fell to the floor, taking her with me.

She squealed loudly and seconds later my bedroom door was crowded with three huge men dressed in suits with their hands on their gun holsters. Tension filled me as I took the men in, my fingers itching for the gun I kept under my pillow.

Damn, I was going to have to remember we weren't in Sicily any longer. Things had been more laid back at the compound in Sicily where we'd lived the last three years with our grandmother. Here, everyone was on red alert since we were home again.

"What happened?" I heard my brother demand and I lifted my head to glare at him. His dark eyes were taking in the room, looking for danger.

Really? The compound walls were surrounded by big—mostly ugly—men with guns. Dogs ran freely on the property and throughout the house, and there was a security system that I was sure came straight from the Secret Service. All of that didn't really matter. I knew that. If someone wanted in, they would get in, but I also knew that, once they did, they would have to face my father's wrath and there weren't very many people in the world who had the balls to do that.

No one was stupid enough to show up at the Vitucci compound to hurt us, yet there my big brother stood, ready to annihilate anything he deemed a threat.

"Make Scarlett get out of bed, Cristiano," Victoria said with a pout as he finally released his hold on his gun and crossed to where we were still tangled together on the floor.

Holding out his hand, he helped her to her feet and then crouched down to grin at me. "Still a grump in the mornings, I see."

"Still a jackass, I see." I reluctantly put my hand in his when he offered it and he stood, pulling me to my feet like I weighed nothing. Compared to him, I didn't. My brother was six foot two of lean muscle. I was five foot eight barefoot, but according to my grandmother, I was too skinny.

He chuckled and glanced down to take me all in. Seeing my choice of pajamas, his chuckle abruptly ended. Remembering the two other men still standing in the doorway of my bedroom, he pulled me behind him and turned to face them. I rolled my eyes. Apparently he had forgotten that I could take care of myself.

"Back to work. Make sure every exit is covered before the meetings start," he barked at the two men whom I instantly recognized. They had worked for my father since before I could remember.

They gave him a curt nod and closed the door as they left. Only then did my brother face me again. "What the fuck are you doing?" His normally nonexistent Italian accent suddenly was now thick and enraged. "You can't go around wearing…"—his hands gestured to my camisole top and panties—"that."

"I wasn't going around," I reminded him, holding on to my irritation by my fingernails. In the three years I'd been away, my brother had obviously forgotten that I wasn't like Victoria and wouldn't put up with his dick-headedness. The last time he'd pissed me off I'd punched him in the throat. "I was in bed. In my own room where I'm supposed to have the privacy to do whatever the hell I please. You're the dumbass who barged in and let your men see me like this." Shaking my head at him, I took the robe my sister handed over and slid my arms inside. Securing it in place, I tied the sash and took Victoria's hand. I was up so I might as well make her happy. "You said something about breakfast?"

She smirked as we moved past Cristiano. "Coming?"

"You can *not* go downstairs like that," he raged behind us as we started down the stairs. "The house will be full of men in an hour. Bad men, Scarlett."

I rolled my eyes at his description of the men my father was meeting with later. Bad men? That was the most hilarious thing I'd heard in forever. Describing the *Cosa Nostra* members as simply bad men was like saying the Ebola virus was a really bad cold. Those guys were not just bad men. They were cold-blooded criminals who ran the city—the damn country—under my father's ever watchful eye.

"Relax," Victoria told him as we reached the bottom of the stairs and he was still trying to get me to go back to my room and change. "We'll eat and then go shopping. That way we won't even be under the same roof as those guys." She released my hand and turned up the wattage of her smile as she looked up at him with her big brown eyes. "Okay?"

I hid my amusement at how well my sister could turn our brother—hell, almost any man—into her minion with just that smile. I had no idea how she did it, because I didn't have that superpower. Our hardass brother turned to putty in her hands right before my eyes.

"You'll have to take some security with you," Cristiano told her as he followed us into the dinning room where the table was already laid out with breakfast foods.

"Of course," she murmured and shot me a wink while his back was turned away. "Whatever you think is best, Cristiano."

"I'd feel better if Ciro or myself could accompany you, Victoria." He sat across from us at the table and poured himself a cup of coffee. "But we'll both be in meetings all day."

Meetings. Right. I liked that they called what was going to happen today *meetings*. It sounded more civil. Political, even.

"We'll be fine," my twin assured him as she delicately buttered her croissant before stuffing half of it in her mouth.

While I watched the two of them, I reached for the pot of espresso and a coffee mug. I poured most of the contents into my mug and then took my time letting the rich coffee wake me up. It was a slow process and one I didn't enjoy. Coffee was the giver of life. Without it I was sure I would have murdered someone by now.

"Good morning, my daughters."

I was thankful the espresso was kicking in when my father walked into the room. I was able to give him a welcoming smile rather than my typical glare that wished whomever it was graced upon to the deepest bowels of hell. He stopped behind Victoria's chair first and pressed a kiss to the top of her head, reminding me of how it had been when we were little girls. Our father might have been the biggest *Cosa Nostra* boss in the country, but when it came to his children, in my eyes he was the best papa in the world.

As I watched Papa, I couldn't help but see the pain that flashed in his eyes as he smiled down at Victoria. For him, Victoria was our mother incarnate and it would always hurt him when he thought of her. He'd both adored and at times hated our mother, but he would always love her. All too soon, he was turning away from her and his pain faded as he gave me a grin that touched my soul. "There you are."

While he was taking in the sight of me, I was doing the same to him. Dressed in a hand-stitched Italian suit, he didn't look like the man I knew could order the death of his enemies with just the flick of his wrist. He just looked like my father, the man who loved me more than life itself. Dark hair, streaked generously with silver, a few wrinkles around his dark eyes that could just as easily be filled with the kind of coldness that made grown men shake in their boots as the warmth and love that was shining out of them right then. Vito was still a very handsome man in his late fifties, but he'd gained a few pounds over the years. His waist was a little thicker than it had been the last time I had seen him.

Without hesitation, I stood and wrapped my arms around his slightly rounded body. “I missed you, Papa.”

His hug didn’t last nearly as long as either of us would have liked. Hell, we could have stood there hugging for hours and it wouldn’t have been long enough for me. There were few people in the world whom I loved as much as I loved my father. To say I was a daddy’s girl was just as much an understatement as calling the guys about to arrive ‘bad men’.

Pulling back, Papa tapped the tip of my nose twice, something he’d always done that told me without words he loved me, and then turned to face my brother. “Is he here?”

I tensed, immediately knowing exactly who ‘he’ was. I glanced at Victoria, who was already watching me closer.

“He had some things to deal with, but he’s on his way now.” Pushing his coffee away, Cristiano stood and gestured toward my robe. “Make her put some clothes on, Papa. She’s practically naked under that thing.”

Vito’s dark eyes assessed my brother dispassionately. “If you can’t control your sister, how will you control your men? Should I be leaving everything to Scarlett instead of you, Cristiano?”

I crossed my arms over my chest, glaring from one Vitucci man to the other. “I’m not someone who can be controlled, Papa. Cristiano could control his men with the snap of his fingers. I, on the other hand, have a brain of my own and don’t need a man to tell me how to use it.”

Vito threw his head back, a deep chuckle making his thick gut shake. "Dear Lord, it's been so boring around here without you, Scarlett." He shook his graying head at me. "But go put some clothes on. Ciro will be here soon and I need all attentions focused on the issues at hand. Not the ones you cause."

"I'm sure Ciro won't even care if I'm dressed like a nun or a tart, Papa." I gave him a kiss on the cheek. "But since Tor will likely murder me in my sleep if I don't hurry so we can go shopping, I'll get ready."

"Shopping?" he boomed. "Who said you could go shopping? I don't want you girls out of the compound for a few days."

Victoria stepped into action, knowing her plans would be put on hold if she didn't start batting her lashes once again. "Cristiano said it wasn't a problem, Papa. We'll be out of the house while your meetings are taking place and we'll have our security with us."

"Victoria, you just returned from Sicily. My men have to get used to you two and your wildness again," Vito tried to argue, but I could tell he was about to give in.

"I promise I'll be on my best behavior, Papa," Victoria murmured demurely, and I could have laughed at the thought of my twin's 'good behavior'. Jesus Christ, my twin was the most mischievous person alive. "And it's only a few days until your birthday. I want to buy you something special."

"Victoria…" She started to pout when his tone said he wasn't going to give in, which had the old man blowing out a harsh sigh. "Fine. If you must go, then go. But be careful. Do not—I repeat—do not run off on your security men. They are there to protect you."

"Yes, Papa." She kissed his other cheek, smiling so brightly the room could have been lit from it alone. "Thank you, Papa."

He sighed again but gave me a wink. "Watch her."

"Yes, Papa."

A throat being cleared had us all turning to find one of Cristiano's men standing in the doorway. He looked like Secret Service, with the earpiece in his ear, and I could easily pick out which side his gun was holstered on. Left side, and probably a Glock from the shape of it. "Adrian Volkov has arrived, sir."

As if someone had turned the air-conditioning on, the temperature in the room seemed to grow cooler and I felt my father stiffening. I'd heard the name Adrian Volkov before. My father didn't clam up when he was talking about work in front of me like he did with Victoria. Volkov was nicknamed 'the wolf' among most of the Mafiosi, but I'd never seen him before. I knew he'd been to prison—both in his home country and in the U.S.—but had no idea what for.

"Show him to my office," Vito informed the man. He didn't speak again until we were alone once more. With his jaw tight, his eyes narrowed to slits and his shoulders straight, he gave Victoria another hug, then gave me a kiss on the cheek before tapping me on the nose twice more. "Get dressed now, Scarlett. I'll have a car and my best men waiting for you in twenty minutes. Please watch over your sister, *passerotta*."

"Always," I assured him.

Chapter 2

Scarlett

Back in my room, I showered and pulled on clothes. I would have rather been pulling on a pair of yoga pants and a T-shirt, but Victoria would have only sent me back to change. My happy-go-lucky twin was a stickler for the proper outfit for every occasion and shopping, to her, was a time to dress up just as much as a party was.

Sitting on the edge of my bed, Victoria crossed her legs and turned her head from left to right, appraising me from every angle. “That dress is cute. Where did you get it?”

I glanced down at the simple white dress with a red rose on the skirt. It was long enough to hide the fact that I had a gun strapped to the inside of my thigh, so it fit both my needs and my sister’s requirements for shopping attire. “I don’t know. It was just in my closet, Tor.” I pulled on a pair of red sandals and then grabbed a hair tie so I could put my hair into a ponytail. "It's probably been in there since we left."

"Well, for something that is three years old, it looks good on you." She stood, smoothing out the wrinkles of her yellow sundress that looked like it had been made to fit her slender yet curvy body.

I was in the process of slipping a pair of small hoops into my ears when I noticed the way she was fidgeting with her dress. "What?" My twin didn't just fidget for no reason. Something was on her mind and she was just waiting for me to make her talk.

"Are you sure you're up for this?" She lifted her lashes and assaulted me with a pair of brown eyes that matched my own, yet held an intensity I didn't know how to mirror.

I turned away, pretending like I didn't know what she was talking about. I didn't want to deal with that shit right now. "When am I ever up for shopping, Tor? I mean, that's your thing. I'd rather be outside, under a shady tree, reading or something."

"Stop it, Scarlett."

Her tone commanded my attention, but I finished securing the earrings before I turned back to her. Putting on a smile that didn't even come close to my twin's normal brightness, I took her hands and gave them a firm squeeze. "I'm fine, Tor. I swear. Seeing Ciro won't be bad. I'll pretend like the last time I saw him never happened and he'll go about being his normal, cold self."

"He's such an emotionless jackass. I want to shoot him with his own gun and see if he's actually human." I preferred her temper to the sadness that had been in her tone just moments before.

Everyone knew I was the temperamental twin, but Victoria was so delightfully happy the majority of the time that they didn't expect her to have a temper under that sweet little voice of hers. Yet it was her they should worry about. With me, what they saw was what they got, and a lot of them were a little scared of me. But when the wrong buttons were pushed, Victoria Vitucci was more dangerous than our father.

My sister had no qualms about getting her hands bloody. She could slit a person's throat and smile sweetly while doing it. I wasn't completely sure our father realized that or not. To him, she was a delicate little flower who should be watched over and protected by everyone, especially me. Because of the severity of her medical condition, he'd always worried after her. The way she reminded him of our mother only made his overprotectiveness of her that much more intense.

My clasp on her hands only tightened. "I'll be fine," I assured her. "I'm not going to chase after Ciro Donati this time around. I learned my lesson. Want to help me move on?"

Her dark eyes brightened once again. "What do you have in mind?"

"Dancing. Lots and lots of dancing." I gave her a sly wink and released her. "Come on. I think I need something sexy to go with the dancing."

"Which club?" Victoria was already making plans, and I was thankful her mind was no longer on Ciro.

I let her do her thing. It was going to take all her scheming to get us out of the house later, but it was better for her to find a way to sneak us out than for her to plan the death of our father's best soldier and *capo*. To be honest, my sister scared the hell out of me when she lost her temper. I was the fearless one, yet she terrified me in that mood. Probably because I'd seen her at work.

Mentally shaking my head, I grabbed my purse and we headed downstairs. It had taken longer than twenty minutes for me to get dressed, so I was sure our father was about to send a search party for us. A search party that would include Cristiano, and I wasn't up to dealing with him again right then.

As we descended the stairs, I heard deep voices speaking in low tones. They were speaking in English, but their accents were so prominent I knew it was a heated conversation without having to listen to what they were saying.

"He's gone MIA. I have all my men looking for him. Every snitch in the city knows that if they see him, I'm to be informed."

I stopped on the last stair as a new voice joined in the conversation. My heart leapt in my chest but I clenched my hands into fists, forcing myself not to openly react to him. Ciro's voice had always had the ability to turn my normally calm self into a mass of hormonally induced anxiety.

"Hannigan has first rights to him for causing all that trouble in California and then bringing it here. Make sure it's taken care of properly, though, Ciro. I don't want any sloppiness," Vito said with the coldness I recognized immediately.

Papa was pissed.

"If he's still on the East Coast, he's a direct threat to the girls," Cristiano interrupted. "Should we still let them go out?"

"Victoria was correct when she said it would be wise that they be out of the house while we take meetings. The less exposure they have to Volkov, the better," Papa assured him.

"I'll send two of my own men with them," Ciro offered. "Or would you like for me to accompany them?"

"Have you even slept?" Cristiano demanded, sounding concerned for his friend. "You look gray around the mouth."

"It was a long night. I grabbed a few hours at the warehouse."

"We shouldn't be listening to this," Victoria whispered at my ear. "If they realized we were, Papa would be angry."

I grimaced, knowing she was right. Even though Papa wasn't nearly as closed-mouthed about business in front of me, the less we knew about what our father did the safer we were, but I was dying to know what Ciro had been up to. And they shouldn't have been having their conversation where anyone could so easily overhear, anyway. They had obviously gotten a little sloppy with where they spoke about business while Victoria and I had been away.

"I think I'll get new shoes," Victoria said, speaking louder than normal, making sure the three men in the next room knew we were approaching. "I'm thinking red."

"Good choice," I murmured.

Cristiano appeared within the next second with Vito and then Ciro right behind him. I kept my focus on my father and brother, refusing to allow myself even a glance at Ciro. If I looked at him right then, I knew I wouldn't be able to hide how much I'd missed him.

The last time I'd seen Ciro played through my head and I swallowed the hurt that tried to choke me. Why was it that this man and only this man had ever been able to touch my dark heart? I would have given him everything if he'd wanted it.

I'd fallen for Ciro when I was eleven. I'd had a crush on him before then. Every girl I knew did, so I couldn't be faulted for having one as well. Ciro had always been a part of my life. I saw him almost every day until I was eighteen. His father was one of Vito's closest friends, and advisor. Papa had been named his godfather at birth, just as his own was Cristiano's. Ciro and Cristiano were best friends practically from birth and Ciro was always at our house.

The day I fell for him, he'd been sitting in the front row of my first—and last—dance recital. His parents were sitting with my father, while he and Cristiano had been off to the side with Dante De Stefano, trying to play it cool while all the girls in my class couldn't stop gaping at them. I'd stepped out onto the stage for my solo and I'd tripped over my own feet in my excitement to show Ciro what I could do.

Tears had instantly filled my eyes in embarrassment and I'd wanted to disappear. From the side of the stage I'd heard the other girls giggling and whispering about me, but they all shut up the moment Ciro jumped up onto the stage beside me and lifted me into his arms like I was a baby.

"Don't cry," he murmured as he'd pressed his lips to my forehead. "You're the best little dancer I've ever seen."

Innocently, I'd fallen hard then and there and I'd kept falling ever since. It was stupid to think he could have felt the same way and I was tired of waiting for him to open his eyes and realize I was all grown up now. When I was eighteen, I'd broken my heart on him for the last time and I'd been all too willing to move to Sicily to live with my grandmother when Papa had suggested we get to know Nona better.

"Finally," Cristiano grumbled. "I was starting to think you two didn't want to leave after all."

"She was in the shower forever," Victoria complained, but she was grinning. "Whose money will I be spending today? Yours, Papa?"

He snorted, but there was an indulgent smile on his face for her. "You would break the bank if you had your way. I should have put you on an allowance from the moment you were born instead of letting you have free rein over my money."

"I have to buy for two most times, Papa. Scarlett would only wear yoga pants and hideous graphic T-shirts if I didn't." She held out her hand, wiggling her fingers at him. "Your cards, please, Papa."

"Don't you have your own?" Cristiano teased, handing over his own credit card before Vito could reach for his wallet.

"Of course," Victoria assured him. "But there is a limit and I have so many outfits to buy. We have nothing to wear for the summer here."

I tried not to roll my eyes at her. Nothing to wear. That was total BS and we all knew it. Our closets were overflowing with dresses that still had the price tags on them. Victoria would donate every one of them though, before filling the racks with new items. She loved working with her charities and donating the contents of her closet—and mine—was just one of the many ways she liked to help out those less fortunate.

"Do you have everything you need?" Vito spoke as Victoria stepped off the last stair to kiss our brother's cheek.

"Of course, Papa."

"I'll take care of her, Papa," I assured him as I stepped forward to kiss his cheek. As I past Ciro I couldn't help but pick up the subtle scent of his aftershave and tried to keep my body from reacting, but I couldn't stop my heart from jumping as that familiar scent brought back so many memories. "Try to be good while we're gone. No shooting anyone," I teased to distract myself.

"I'll try to hold the urge, *passerotta*," Papa said with a straight face.

"Am I interrupting?"

I felt all three men tense before I could turn to see who had spoken. I thought I heard Ciro curse under his breath, but I didn't chance looking at him to confirm if I was right or not. Instead I kept my eyes on my father. The way his face became completely emotionless told me he considered the newcomer an enemy. Turning slowly, I let my eyes fall on the man standing in the doorway that led to my father's office at the back of the first floor of the house.

It was hard to say which part of the man caught my attention first. He was a few inches shorter than Ciro, who was a beast at six foot six. His black hair was cut short, and there was a dark scruff on his face that suggested he kept it that way. His suit was handmade and expensive, but no more Italian than he was. He was leaner than Ciro, but thicker muscled than Cristiano. The tattoos on his hands looked like gang ink, and I found myself wondering if he had others elsewhere.

His dark eyes went from my father to me. I watched as he ran his gaze from the top of my head to the tip of my shoes, then back again. His appraisal was full of interest, but I was unaffected. Seeing the indifference in my eyes, he turned his gaze to Victoria. The interest that he'd had for me seemed to double in a blink of an eye and the room seemed to grow marginally warmer as Victoria actually stared back with her own interest evident.

"These must be your daughters," the newcomer who had to be Adrian Volkov said in a voice that had the slightest Russian accent.

The three other men remained close-mouthed, but my twin stepped forward as if they weren't even there. "I'm Victoria," she murmured as she offered him her hand.

"Adrian." His voice deepened when he touched her fingers, his dark eyes flashing with a desire that scorched even me.

I watched with narrowed eyes as Victoria seemed to shiver and left her hand in his. Their eyes stayed locked for a long moment as if they were trapped in their own little world, before Cristiano stepped forward and pulled Victoria back.

His jaw tense, he pushed Victoria toward me, then turned back to our guest. "Shall we?"

Adrian followed Victoria's every step until she reached my side. Only then did he turn that predatory gaze on my brother. As the two men stared each other down, I could tell that the rumors were true about Volkov. He was a very dangerous man. Then, just as quickly as that dangerous gleam had flashed in his dark eyes, it was replaced with a neutral expression and his lips lifted into a cool smile.

"Lead the way."

I glanced at Papa as Cristiano disappeared, trying to judge his reaction. Vito's face remained completely impassive though, until we heard the door to his office close. Then his mask of indifference fell and I saw the anger in his eyes. I couldn't ever remember him looking at either Victoria or me with that look before, but right then he was incensed with my twin.

"Have you lost your damn mind?" he raged as he took hold of Victoria's arm and turned her to face him. She'd been so lost in watching Volkov walk away she hadn't even realized what awaited her until right then. "That is Adrian Volkov. He is a violent felon. You are not—I repeat—are not to speak to him ever again."

"Papa…" Victoria started to argue, but he only tightened his hold on her arm painfully. I watched as her eyes narrowed, too shocked by everything to move.

What the fuck had just happened? Volkov had appeared and tossed everyone upside down. I wasn't sure I liked it.

Victoria swallowed hard and then nodded. "I understand, Papa."

Chapter 3

Ciro

If the urge to kill Adrian Volkov hadn't already been burning through my veins, it became an inferno the second I'd watched that Russian fucker run his eyes down Scarlett's body. The only thing that had saved him was Scarlett standing there to witness his murder.

I doubted she would have blinked if I had. Scarlett Vitucci was so much like her father, I knew she wouldn't have flinched if I'd pulled out my Beretta and shot that motherfucker where he stood. I had no desire to show her that side of me, though. I didn't want her to see what kind of a monster most me were so afraid of.

Vito released Victoria and turned his cold glare on me. "Make sure they get off safely, Ciro. You said you were sending two of your men with them. Your best men."

I inclined my head. "Yes, sir."

"Scarlett, watch over your sister." His coldness seemed to disappear when he lifted his hand and tapped her lovingly on the nose, twice. "Be safe, *passerotta*."

"Yes, Papa," she murmured, and I had to clench my jaw to keep from reacting to her slightly husky voice. Fuck me, her voice was like a softly caressing hand across my cock.

Vito shot me another hard look, one that said a thousand different things, and turned to follow Cristiano. I waited until he was out of sight before turning to face the twins. How was it that Scarlett and Victoria were identical in every visual way, yet when I looked at Victoria my body remained completely unaffected? As I took her in, I didn't feel anything except maybe a brotherly sort of affection.

Shifting my gaze to the older twin, my heart contracted uncomfortably and my dick came to life immediately. Her long red hair was pulled back into a simple ponytail. There was no trace of makeup on her alabaster skin, and her light brown eyes were looking at something behind me. I would have given my last breath to have her look at me—to have her eyes devour me as they once had—but knew it was better for everyone if she didn't.

"You look as if you haven't slept in days, Ciro," Victoria commented as she turned her full attention on me.

I shrugged, dismissing her concern. In truth, I hadn't slept in two days, but I wasn't about to explain that to either of them. "Shall we?" I moved to open the front door. On the other side, two men in suits stood at the ready. I gave them each a curt nod, but they didn't move from their posts.

In the driveway, Vito's Town Car was already waiting. The car looked like a typical sedan, but the windows were bullet-proof. Behind the wheel, a man with an entire arsenal of guns and knives sat, ready to protect the Vitucci twins with his life if he had to. Two other men were already standing by the back passenger door, waiting for Scarlett and Victoria.

Three men. Not nearly enough in my opinion. Fuck, twenty men wouldn't be enough to protect Scarlett if it were up to me. Gritting my teeth, I pulled out my phone and snapped a command to the man who answered. I trusted all of my men, but Desi was the only one I would entrust with Scarlett's life.

Without answering me, he appeared from beside the house where he normally waited for me when I was at the compound. Beside him was Paco. The two were brothers, and I knew they would keep Scarlett safe. Vito's two men didn't even blink when my guys stepped up beside them. It might have been three years since they'd had to worry about protecting the twins, but they knew not to question any extra men being added to their security detail.

Victoria stepped around me and descended the steps to the car without another word, but I felt Scarlett pause just behind me. Stilling myself to look at her, I slowly turned to find her eyeing the compound grounds in front of her. The compound was over thirty acres, with a wall up around the borders of the property. Men patrolled it day and night, but the men had learned to fade into the background, and all anyone really saw was the beauty of the many trees, tended lawns and gardens, and the long, stone driveway.

Scarlett's eyes seemed to drink all of that in as she stood on the top step. I watched as a small smile teased at her luscious lips and her lashes drifted down as if trying to savor every little detail. She was so damn beautiful, my heart virtually stopped just watching her like that.

"I'll never get tired of this sight," she murmured, and I wasn't sure if she was speaking to herself or if she was actually gracing me with conversation. "No matter the season, this will always be my favorite view. I've missed it."

"You didn't like Sicily?" I asked before I could stop myself.

She shrugged without turning her gaze away from the scenery. "I loved it there. It was beautiful and it was wonderful getting to know some of my extended family. But…" Her brown eyes turned to me, looking at me for the first time. I saw the way her pupils dilated, knew she was just as affected at the sight of me as I was. "There's nothing like home, you know?"

Before I could question what I was doing, I reached for her. Clasping her hand gently in my own, I lifted it to my lips and pressed a kiss to her knuckles. "I do know." Slowly, I released her, mentally cursing myself for the need that had consumed me to touch her. Ten fucking minutes and I was already finding it hard to keep my hands to myself. I knew if I didn't stop I would become addicted to the feel of her softness under my fingertips. "It's good to have you home, Scarlett."

Her eyes were turned to her now free hand, her lips slightly parted as if she was panting. I counted the erratic beats of her heart from the pulse at the base of her throat. Seeing how easily I could get her to respond only made my need for her twice as bad.

"You should go now," I told her when she just stood there, as if frozen in place. "I'm sure you have lots of shopping to do."

Her head snapped up, her eyes narrowed in a mixture of hurt and anger, and I reminded myself that I wanted her to be pissed with me. Her hating me was easier to deal with. It made it easier to walk away.

Liar.

It wasn't easier for me. Not even a little. Yet for her, it was simple. She didn't speak as she walked down to the car and let Desi help her into the back seat. She sat, and kept her eyes trained straight ahead. Desi shut the door and I was able to pull my gaze from her.

"Keep them safe," I commanded. Keep *her* safe, was what I meant but would never say aloud.

The men climbed into the car and I watched until it had disappeared through the gates before going back into the house. Only then did I let thoughts of Volkov reenter my mind. As I went past Vito's men on my way to his office, they paused to let me pass, keeping even more distance between themselves and me than they normally would have.

I had that effect on most of the men I worked with—and even more that I didn't. From the age of seventeen I'd been one of Vito's soldiers. I'd followed my father's lead into the *Cosa Nostra*, but it hadn't been the fact that I was Benito Donati's son that had made men start to fear me back then. Benito was Vito's *consigliere,* sure, but I'd proven myself over and over again, not just to Vito, but his *caporegimes* as well, that I was worthy of being one of his soldiers.

Now I was a *capo* with my own men to command, but more often than not I was a soldier, carrying out orders that Vito only ever trusted me with. I could never wash away the blood that now stained my hands and it was one of the reasons I knew Scarlett would be better off with someone else.

Fuck. I wanted to put my fist through something when that reminder flashed through my head.

I entered the office without pausing to knock. Instead, I walked in, crossed to where Adrian Volkov was standing casually by the window, and grabbed him by the collar. Slamming him up against the wall, I got in his face, my rage vibrating through my entire body. "You ever look at her like that again and I will send your sister your head giftwrapped with your entrails."

The only reaction Volkov gave of anger was his eyes narrowing. "Is she yours?"

I didn't answer. Scarlett was mine, but I could never claim her. To do so would be like putting a neon target on her back. My enemies were dying to find a weakness in me, so I would never let them know that Scarlett was my only one. Even if that weren't such a huge risk, she deserved better than a man with so much blood on his hands. Volkov had just as much, if not more.

I would kill him before I let him touch her.

"Easy, Ciro." Cristiano put his hand on my shoulder and gave it a hard squeeze. "Volkov knows to stay away from Victoria."

Victoria.

Fuck that shit. I didn't give two fucks about Victoria. It was Scarlett I would gut him for.

Releasing him, I straightened my tie and stepped back, making my face go completely blank. It was time to get to work. I'd deal with Volkov later.

The Russian fixed his suit jacket, his face just as impassive as my own. "Back to business?" Vito gave a single nod. "As I was saying, I have eyes on the entire Santino family. All except for Carlo Jr. He's a ghost as of yesterday."

That wasn't news to me. The Santino family was a West Coast based *Casa Nostra* that wanted to set up shop in New York. They didn't have the connections or the money to take over Vito's territory, but that hadn't stopped them from trying. Jr had tried to marry into the Morgan family, which held about as much political pull in some circles as the Kennedys did. With their help he could have set up camp in Connecticut and slowly made his name known in New York.

Jr's plans were now shattered, which was one of the reasons I hadn't gotten any sleep and was now running on fumes.

"So we have no idea if that bastard is still in the area or if he's gone back to California." Cristiano thrust his hands into his pants pockets and glared out the window Volkov was still standing by.

"He's not in California," I assured him. "The Angel's Halo MC has eyes on the Santino compound. If Jr had shown up I would've known by now."

"You're so sure of that?" Volkov lifted a bored eyebrow at me. "Aren't the MC looking for Jr too?"

"They wouldn't make a move on him without informing me. The MC's VP is in Connecticut as we speak. Their president won't touch Jr without Hawk Hannigan's say so. Not after what has happened to his woman."

"Will she live?" Vito asked from his seat behind his desk.

"The blood poisoning is bad, but the doctors have assured my people that she should make a full recovery."

"Good. A pissed-off gang of bikers is not something any of us need storming around this city." Vito turned his blank stare on Volkov. "I'll expect regular reports from you or your second-in-command. Santino is all of our problems and until we get him neutralized none of us will know peace."

"Agreed." Volkov moved away from the window. "You will have my full cooperation regarding this matter."

"Wait," Vito commanded in a tone that few men had ever ignored, when Volkov looked as if he was going to leave. The Russian paused and looked at Vito, his face blank. "Stay away from my daughter, or Ciro's earlier promise will become a reality."

"I'll make sure to make Anya aware of the possibility." With that he walked away.

"That could be a problem," Cristiano muttered once he was gone.

"If it becomes one, I'll handle it," I promised my friend. With pleasure.

"No," Vito said after a moment. "No, let's see what happens first."

"You know he will make a move on her, Papa."

My head felt like it was about to explode. I knew they meant Victoria, but all I could see was the the way Volkov had looked at Scarlett and I wanted to tear that fucker apart.

"Yes, I do know." His eyes darkened. "Have him followed. Tell your men to keep their distance though. As I said, let's see what happens."

Chapter 4

Scarlett

When the taxi pulled up outside of a club I was unfamiliar with, I knew instantly that Victoria was up to something. There was a line two blocks long of people trying to get in. Three bouncers stood by the ropes that kept everyone back, only allowing a few in at a time as more people left.

Shooting my smiling twin a glare, I didn't immediately turn when one of the bouncers stepped forward and opened the back door for me.

"Is this what I think it is, Tor?"

She gave me a sly grin. "You said to pick a club, so I picked a club."

"A club that's probably owned by Adrian Volkov. Papa's head will explode if he finds out." I didn't even think about how big the mess would be if he found out Victoria and I had snuck out of the compound. We'd done it hundreds of times in our teens and had only gotten caught twice, thanks to my twin's genius planning.

Twice was enough for me to dread my father finding out again.

"Adrian doesn't own Iron Hand," she assured me, and I started to relax. "His sister, Anya, does."

Damn it.

"Miss?"

I bit back a curse as I finally gave the bouncer my hand and stepped out of the taxi. With the heels I was wearing, I needed his help to stand up straight. Why I had let my sister talk me in to them, I still had no clue. I'd been weak after my exchange with Ciro earlier and had been even less involved in the shopping process than usual.

Victoria slid across the bench seat and let him help her out next. Her heels were just as dangerous as my own but, unlike me, she walked like she had been born in them. Giving the bouncer a coy smile, she turned her head, letting her long red curls fall over one shoulder. "Volkov is expecting us," she told him.

Wait—she was? When had Victoria spoken to her?

"Name?" the big man growled, and I stepped closer to my sister, wanting to put myself between her and the possible dangers this guy represented.

"Victoria," she murmured in a voice that was soft and husky.

I saw the bouncer actually shiver. How the hell did she do that? She could bend any man to her will with just a simple word, and I wanted to know how. Maybe if I knew how, I could have convinced Ciro years ago that we were meant to be together. I realized I'd been wrong but, hell, I couldn't stop thinking about the 'what ifs'.

Lifting his hand, the bouncer touched the communication device in his ear. "What should I do with Victoria?" His eyes didn't give away what whoever was on the other end was saying. "Yes, ma'am."

The man moved to the entrance and held the door open for us. "Go straight in. Miss Volkov is in a meeting right now, but she will join you at the bar on the second floor when she's finished."

As soon as we stepped into the club my senses went into overload. There were different colored lights everywhere, flashing to the beat of the music flooding through the club provided by a skilled DJ on a platform on the first floor. Sweet incense filled me with a feeling of calm even as I dreaded taking my next step inside. The space inside could easily hold two thousand people, and I was pretty sure there were at least half that in attendance right then.

Huge couches filled every corner where large groups were both sitting and lying as they enjoyed drinks—and probably stronger, more dangerous things—with friends. On the second floor, I could see the bar where a smaller crowd of people were spread out. The two extra-large men standing by the stairs that led to the second floor told me exactly why those numbers were so much smaller than that on the first floor.

Victoria took my hand and urged me toward the staircase. The trip was long and we had to weave through several drunken dancers before we reached our destination. Seeing her, the two guards stepped forward. "Any weapons?" the one on my left asked us both.

I shook my head just as Victoria did but, unlike her, I was completely lying. I had a knife strapped to the inside of my inner right thigh and a derringer strapped to my left. Both had been a gift from Ciro when I was seventeen, when Victoria and I'd been caught at a club in Manhattan for the second time. He'd known we would probably do it again, and he'd wanted to make sure I was protected if I did. I never went out without either of them now.

Thinking about the friendship we'd had back then made my stomach tighten and my chest ache with longing for how it had been in the old days. Fuck, I missed him so damn much.

The one on my right grasped Victoria's wrist and pulled her closer, making me stiffen. "We have to check for sure, miss." His quiet voice didn't fit his overly large body and I almost laughed because it was so surprising.

"Does it look like I could hide a weapon?" she snapped at him as his hands started to lift to touch her shoulders. I widened my stance, ready to reach for my gun and not giving a damn who saw me waving it in these two fuckheads' faces. "I have maybe two feet of fabric on and all my assets are on display. Do you think these girls aren't real?" Her hands touched her breasts, lifting them.

From behind me I heard a harsh hiss. The bouncer followed the movement of Victoria's hands and I saw the interest light up his eyes. If he touched her, his brains would be splattered on the wall behind him before he could take his next breath. I'd kill the sonofabitch and wouldn't have a minute of regret.

Before I could even move, the bouncer was backed into the wall beside the stairs, his face turning purple as Adrian Volkov squeezed the life out of him. "Touch her again. I dare you."

"I was just following protocol," the man was able to wheeze out. "Miss Volkov said…"

"Do I look like I give a fuck what my sister said? These two are the exception." His grip tightened. "Understand?"

Unable to speak at all now, the bouncer could only nod. Volkov slowly released his hold on the man and turned around, but his gaze went straight to Victoria. The rage that had been vibrating off him only a moment before faded in the next blink of his eyes. "I should have known you would be trouble." His accent was prominent now, all the anger gone from his face as he watched my sister through his thick lashes. "I wasn't expecting you to be so brave, *kotyonok*."

It took me a second to realize what he'd just called her because my Russian wasn't nearly as good as Victoria's was. *Kitten*. It fit her, considering I thought I actually heard Victoria purr as he grasped her hand and pulled her closer. Volkov had to be some kind of magician or something, because my sister didn't just act like this. Ever. She was incredibly feminine, but she'd never been the kind of girl who lost her mind the second a hot guy looked twice at her. She'd never had a crush, never really noticed guys because most of the ones we were around on a daily basis either worked for our father or were related to us.

She was under his spell, but as I watched her lean into his touch when he lifted a hand to cup her chin, I realized she'd never looked so happy in her life. My happy sister, the only one who could shine a light on my darkness, was glowing as bright as the sun at midday right then.

Then and there I knew it didn't matter how angry Papa got over her being with Volkov. I wouldn't let anyone stand in her way.

***

Volkov led us upstairs and to a back corner that was completely deserted. As he sat on the long, wide couch with dark pillows, I realized it was his special corner. Almost like they had been part of the woodwork, two large men in suits appeared at each end of the couch.

Still holding Victoria's hand, he pulled her down beside him and she went willingly. I sat several feet away from them, wanting to give them some privacy yet wanting to be close enough to protect her if Volkov turned out to be a total creep. My fingers still itched to put a bullet in the bouncer who had touched my sister.

A waitress dressed in a simple white button-down and a short black skirt appeared at Volkov's side. "Champagne, I think," he told the girl without bothering to look at her.

"No." Victoria shook her head and smiled as she forced her eyes away from him to look up at the waitress, who seemed almost surprised at the attention. "Vodka. Bring us a bottle and four shot glasses. Anya is joining us, right?"

Volkov's surprise showed in his eyes for only half a second before he was tossing his head back and laughing out loud. "I can see now you will keep me on my toes, *kotyonok.* I like that. I like that a lot, actually."

I sat back and tried to relax as the waitress walked away to get the vodka. "Not too much, Tor," I cautioned her quietly.

She had to be more careful than others when she was drinking because of her health. If her blood sugar levels fell too low, it would be hard to tell if she was drunk or not because the signs mirrored someone who'd had too much to drink. I was always watching over her to make sure that she didn't take things too far.

She gave a nod but didn't say anything as she kept her full attention on Volkov. Apparently she didn't want to talk about her illness in front of her new friend. "So you and my father… Is there a reason for the tension?"

The amusement drained out of his face and his eyes turned cool. "You could say we have recently become reluctant allies."

Reluctant allies. Interesting acuity. That was the most diplomatic way to describe having to do my father's bidding that I'd ever heard. Volkov was smart, I'd give him that. I glanced at the ink on his hands.

ВОЛК

It took me a second to decode the Russian text on four fingers of his left hand. *Wolf.* Fitting. I saw the five dots closer to his wrist on the same hand. That meant he'd done time. There were other markings but I wasn't sure of their meanings. I could only assume it was what he'd been convicted of or some kind of code to tell others what his position was.

"So you don't deal with Papa often?" Victoria was still trying to get Volkov to talk.

He shrugged and I was glad to see he didn't fall under her spell easily. "Often enough. Vito and I have an understanding. Cristiano and I? Not so much." He grinned. "My sister says it's because we are too much alike."

"You are."

My head lifted at the sound of the new voice and I took Anya Volkov in for the first time. She was beyond beautiful, with her long, dark hair. She had the prettiest porcelain skin I'd ever seen and her big, blue eyes stood out amid her other features. Her lips were full and crimson with a light gloss coating them. I was sure she was younger than her brother by several years and put her age at twenty-five at the most. If I'd been a vain sort of female, I would have been instantly jealous of Anya and her perfect body. Instead, I felt an instant connection with her that made me wonder if we could possibly become good friends.

Unsmiling, Anya took both me and Victoria in. The expression on her face was detached, but her eyes couldn't completely hide how much she was assessing the two of us. After a moment she tilted her head to the side. She pointed a finger at my sister. "Victoria." The finger then went to me. "Scarlett."

It was normal for strangers to get who we were wrong the first time they met us, but Anya's perspicacity was strong. Victoria beamed up at her and stood. Even if she wasn't wearing heels, she would have been taller than Anya. Victoria towered over her as she moved to embrace the other woman. "I knew I would like you when we spoke earlier."

"Let's say I was intrigued when Cristiano Vitucci's sister called out of the blue to request an invite to my humble club." Her lips lifted in a bitchy half-smirk as she glanced at her brother, who hadn't moved. "Now I understand perfectly. Why am I not surprised, Adrian?"

He only grasped Victoria's hand and pulled her back down beside him, as if he couldn't stand to have her so far away. Anya rolled her eyes at him, but the waitress returned with the vodka and shot glasses. Taking the tray from the girl, she dismissed her and then sat down between me and Victoria.

"I would have picked tequila, myself, but to each their own." She poured four shots, handed two to her brother and Victoria before offering me one. Sitting back, she tapped her glass to mine. "To new and unexpected friendships."

I found myself grinning at her dry tone. Yes, I was really going to like this woman. "*Salute.*"

Chapter 5

Ciro

After the meetings with Vito all morning, I'd gone to check on my mother and had ended up falling asleep in her den for a few hours. By the time I'd gotten up, it was dinnertime and I had stayed to eat to make her happy.

With a full stomach and a few hours' rest, I knew I wasn't going to get any sleep that night. I could have gone home or out to Connecticut to check on my MC connections, but instead I found myself back at the Vitucci compound. I mentally cursed myself for going back, but I couldn't have stopped myself even if I'd wanted to. The need to be closer to Scarlett was too strong for me to fight it.

Vito was out with my father, the twins had apparently called it an early night, but Cristiano was in the family room watching an MMA fight. Any other time he would have been front and center at such a big fight, but because of the current Santino issues he was sticking closer to home.

I took one of the beers he offered and dropped down at the other end of the couch. The thing I liked about Cristiano so much was that we didn't have to talk to communicate. We could just sit there and watch two men tear each other apart for sport and be comfortable with the silence. We'd become friends because it was expected of us. He'd become my brother because he was the only person who understood me.

We sat there together through the entire event before either of us spoke.

"Stone is still a powerhouse," Cristiano commented as the camera zoomed in on the man who was still the heavyweight champion after a match that had been brutal and bloody. "I'd like to get him to fight New Years Eve here in New York. Think he would be interested?"

"If the money is right, I wouldn't see an issue." I lifted my third beer to my lips and took a long swallow. With each passing second I grew more tense. The beer wasn't helping me control the need to climb the stairs and knock on Scarlett's bedroom door.

"I offered him five million for a single fight last Christmas. He refused."

"So sweeten the pot," I suggested and set my now empty bottle on the coffee table with the other empties. "And if that doesn't work, talk to his wife."

"She's not his wife." He reached for the remote and turned the TV off. "And from what I heard, she's a little firecracker. It might be interesting to introduce myself to her."

I paused in the process of opening my fourth beer. Cristiano had a weakness for beautiful things—women included. Fuck, especially women. I could easily see him trying to move in on the MMA fighter's woman and getting his head bashed in by the guy's fists in the process. Stone wouldn't care who the hell Cristiano was. "Keep your hands clean, Cristiano," I warned him.

"For fuck's sake, I said introduce myself," he muttered. "Relax, *fratello*."

"Let the professionals handle the haggling. You have plenty of entertainment around here." I lifted the fresh beer to my lips and swallowed thirstily.

Cristiano shrugged. "For now."

Shaking my head, I stood. "You're an idiot. One day you'll meet your undoing and I'm going to laugh when she twists you into knots."

"Says the man who refuses to acknowledge that he's already met his own undoing," my friend muttered, and I stiffened. "Deny it all you want, but Scarlett would be better off—"

"She'd be better off with a two-story house in the suburbs with a white picket fence and three kids running around. I'm not worthy of her," I snarled at him. Just the thought of Scarlett as a mother made my chest tighten. She would be a great mom, but those kids would never be mine. I didn't want kids. Ever. I wouldn't subject an innocent little baby to being my child. "Now drop it." I had thought about slitting his throat more than once since I'd realized my friend knew my secret. Right then, the idea held even more appeal.

He lifted his hands in surrender. "Keep telling yourself that. Whatever helps you sleep at night. Meanwhile, my sister will find a spineless weasel to marry and give her those three kids."

"Remind me again why I haven't killed you yet?" I downed the rest of the nearly full bottle of beer.

"I'm still wondering that myself." He grinned and slowly got to his feet. "I'm tired. I'll see you tomorrow."

"If I don't slit your throat in your sleep," I muttered half to myself.

"Feel free to take your usual room," he called over his shoulder with a chuckle, possibly the only man alive who didn't take my threats seriously. "Maybe you'll grow a pair and find yourself in Scarlett's room instead."

Without thinking about what I was doing, I threw the now empty bottle at his head. He stepped through the doorway just as the bottle shattered against the doorframe. Heavy feet came running, but Cristiano only chuckled deeper. "Get a broom and clean up the mess," he told the guards who had come in search of the reason for the noise.

"Fuck," I muttered to myself and ran my hands down my face.

I shouldn't have come back to the compound. Shaking my head at the ideas flashing through my head after Cristiano's taunts, I went into the kitchen to make some coffee. I'd drink a cup and then head home. At least that's what I kept telling myself as I made the coffee, but my eyes kept going to the back stairs that led straight to Scarlett's room.

The coffeemaker was still dripping when I thought I heard a thump upstairs. Frowning, I headed for the stairs. Halfway up, I heard a giggle, followed by a groan, and I increased my pace.

"Are you trying to get us caught?" a voice I recognized all too well muttered as I grew closer to Victoria's partially shut bedroom door.

"I think I had one too many shots of vodka with Anya," a second voice said before the giggles came again. "Do you think she likes us?"

I stiffened at the mention of that particular name. Anya? Anya Volkov? I took the last step and quietly walked down the hall toward where I was sure I'd heard the two voices coming from.

"Don't worry about if she did or didn't," Scarlett commanded. "Get in bed, Tor. I'm exhausted."

"I really like him." Victoria's voice was softer now and I stopped just outside of her bedroom as I listened to the twins moving around.

"Really? I couldn't tell." Scarlett's tone was dry. "Hold still, Tor. I'm going to hurt your arm if you keep doing that…Tor!"

"I can dress myself," the other twin mumbled.

"Of course you can," Scarlett soothed. "It will be quicker if I help, though. Just let me check your sugar levels. Then you can go to sleep and dream about your Russian wolf."

My hands clenched into fists as I waited for her to finish helping her sister. They had snuck out. I should have known they would. How many times had I told Scarlett that it was dangerous for her to leave the compound without security with her and Victoria? They hadn't gone just anywhere either. From the mention of Anya, I figured they had gone to Iron Hand and it was more than obvious to me that Adrian had been in attendance.

Had Scarlett wanted to go out and meet the Russian? Was she interested? Fuck, I'd gut that sonofabitch if he touched her.

"Sleep tight, Tor." I heard her footsteps bringing her closer to the door.

"Night, Scarlett. Love you."

The bedroom door was pulled open and Scarlett stepped out into the hall. She didn't look toward the stairs as she closed the door and then headed for her own room across the hall.

"Enjoy your night out?"

She gasped and jumped at the sound of my voice. Turning to face me, she put a hand over her chest "You scared me," she accused, her brown eyes flashing fire.

My eyes skimmed over her, taking in the little black dress she was wearing with heels so high the top of her head actually came to my chin. The dress was low cut, showing off an enticing view of her tits. The skirt went almost to her knees; which I guess I should have been thankful for. If she'd been walking around New York with her ass practically hanging out of her dress I probably would have gone on a damn killing spree to eradicate anyone who had seen her like that.

I took a step toward her and watched as her eyes dilated with a reaction that paralleled my own to her. "Where did you go?"

The tip of her tongue darted out of her mouth to dampen her bottom lip. "Just to a club," she said with a shrug. "We were fine, Ciro. I have the gun you gave me."

"Oh, yeah?" My gaze ate up the sight of her and I tried to curb my need to reach out and take what I wanted so damn bad. "Where is it?"

"Strapped to the inside of my thigh," she assured me. "Along with my knife."

Jesus Christ.

Without realizing I was doing it, I took another step closer to her, then another. I wanted to see the gun I'd given her strapped to her creamy thighs. The dark color of the metal against the perfect alabaster of her skin—it got me hard just imagining it. I wanted those long legs of hers to wrap around my waist while I dived into her with that gun still strapped to her thigh.

Before I lost complete control and did just that, I stopped a few inches from her. "You were with Volkov, weren't you?"

She didn't even flinch at the coldness of my tone when I'd seen grown-ass men piss themselves in the face of it. Scarlett knew I would never hurt her though. "Does it matter? We were just having fun, Ciro. There's no crime in that."

"He's dangerous, Scarlett. You know nothing about him." I turned away from her, my hands fisting at my sides so I wouldn't touch her. "Don't go near him again. I don't want you to get hurt."

She crossed her arms over her chest, making the globes of her tits lift, almost as if they were begging me to look—to touch them. "He's no more dangerous than you or Cristiano. He seems like a nice guy. If I want to see him again, I will."

"The fuck you will." Jealousy raged through me and I couldn't have held back then if I'd tried to. I reached for her and pushed her back against the wall beside her bedroom door. Her lips fell open, a soft breath escaping her that felt like a caress down my spine.

"Ciro." Her hands pushed against my chest, but I saw the need rising in her eyes, saw the way her cheeks darkened with a desire she had no more control over than I did. "Wh-what are you doing?"

I had no answer for her. I wasn't thinking. The rage I felt, the jealousy, was eating me alive and all I wanted to do was brand her in every way imaginable as my own. "Stay away from Volkov," I muttered as I lowered my head and skimmed my nose down her throat. She smelled so damn good. It was a sweet, floral kind of scent that intoxicated me faster than alcohol ever could. Scarlett inhaled shakily and my hold tightened on her hip. "I'll kill him if you don't."

Her fingers clenched around the material of my shirt, trying to pull me closer. "Why?" she demanded. "Why would you kill him? It's not like you care if I hook up with him."

"Try it and see," I growled at her ear and felt her shiver.

"Ciro…"

"I'm completely serious, Scarlett." I pressed my lips to the shell of her ear. Fuck, she tasted even better than she smelled. "If you want Volkov dead, see him again. I dare you."

She pressed her forehead into my throat. "If you would open your eyes for two seconds you would know that I'm not interested in Adrian Volkov." She released her hold on my shirt and pushed me back half a step. I went willingly, unable to even think about not giving her what she wanted. Lifting her eyes to mine, she shook her head. "Victoria has a thing for him, not me. The guy I want keeps saying he doesn't want me, then goes apeshit when he thinks I'm into someone else."

I clenched my jaw. "I'm no good for you, Scarlett."

She shrugged. "So you keep telling me. Don't worry though, Ciro." She turned away from me, but not before I saw the flash of pain in her brown eyes. Before I could open my mouth—to call her back, to apologize, to do who the fuck knew what—her hand was reaching for the door. "I'm starting to believe you."

Chapter 6

Scarlett

A weird sound coming from my phone pulled me out of a deep sleep. Groaning, because I just wanted the noise to stop so I could go back to sleep, I reached for the phone. Cracking one eye open so I could see how to turn it off, my gaze caught the sight of the name flashing across the screen.

I closed my eyes and opened them again, taking another look. The name was still the same. Hell. Frowning, I hit connect, too curious to think about sleep any longer. "I thought you Russians could handle vodka better than you did last night. Three shots and you called it quits."

Anya Volkov snorted in my ear. "It's called running a business, little Italian princess. I had to keep my head clear to deal with work."

"Sure," I yawned. "You just knew I'd outdrink you."

"Keep telling yourself that." Anya blew out a long breath and I got the feeling that whatever was going to come out of her mouth was full of reluctance. I pushed the hair back from my face as I waited. "I have a favor to ask."

I glanced at the clock beside my bed. Two seventeen in the afternoon. At least Victoria had let me sleep. That was a rare occurrence, and quickly got me wondering what the hell she was doing that she didn't want me to know about. Sighing, I turned my attention back to Anya. "You can ask it, that doesn't mean I'll be able fulfill it."

There was no way in hell I was going to agree to give her a favor without knowing what it was. I might have liked the little Russian immediately, but that didn't mean I was stupid. I got the feeling that Anya was just as dangerous as her brother.

"I want you to keep your sister away from my brother."

I sat up straight in bed, anger at the steel in her voice already boiling through my veins. "Excuse me?"

Another long sigh. "You heard me, Scarlett. Your sister has no idea what she's in store for if she gets involved with Adrian. I love my brother—really, I do. He's the most important person in my life. Without him I would have nothing. But I don't want to see Victoria get hurt."

I couldn't believe what she was saying. The night before, Anya had seemed to like Victoria. Had even looked approvingly at the couple as the night had progressed. Had I read it wrong? Now she wanted me to step in and keep them apart? I couldn't—wouldn't—do that to my sister unless there was a good enough reason. “Why?” I bit out. “Why do you want her to stay away from him?”

There was a long pause on her end before she muttered something in Russian I didn’t completely catch. “I can’t tell you without betraying my brother’s confidence. But if you care about your sister, you will keep her away from Adrian.” Another pause but I didn’t try to break the tension that was building. Right then I wanted to tear Anya’s hair out by the handful and shove it down her throat before I broke her pretty little neck. “If you love your sister as much as I love my brother, you won’t want to see her heart broken.”

“I’m not going to stand in her way if Adrian is who Tor wants,” I told her, angry her elusiveness. “Unless you tell me my sister’s life is in danger, then I’m not doing shit to keep her away from him.”

Anya’s laugh held no humor. “It’s not her life you need to worry about, *myshka*. It’s her heart, and in the long run, that’s more important. I like her, Scarlett. For her own good, keep her away.”

Before I could blast into her, the phone went dead in my ear. Pissed off, I tossed my phone on the bed and got up. I had no idea what the hell was going on with fucking Adrian Volkov but I was going to find out. Until then, I wasn’t going to stand between him and Victoria.

But if he did hurt her, I’d personally put a bullet right between his eyes.

Cursing under my breath, I quickly showered and dressed before heading downstairs. I wouldn’t say anything to my sister about Anya’s call, not until I found out what was up with the Russian. *If* I found out anything. It could have just been Anya being a manipulative bitch. Maybe I'd gotten it wrong the night before and she hadn't liked Victoria. I could normally read a person pretty well, but Anya was different.

Knowing better than to ask my father or even Cristiano personally, I went searching for the first person I knew would hopefully give me answers. Before I'd left for Sicily, Ciro had been my closest confidant, second to no one. I'd gone to him with everything and he had dropped everything to help me. If I had a problem, he would either give me advice or deal with it himself. That had all changed when I'd left, but right then it was the only option I had. After the night before I wasn't sure if I was strong enough to be alone with him, but I had to find out if Adrian Volkov could hurt my sister or not.

As I descended the stairs, I saw Cristiano talking to one of his men. His head turned when he heard my footsteps and he dismissed the other man with a curt order in Italian. That curtness was gone as he turned around, and not for the first time I was surprised by how easily he could turn off his coldness. For all the bickering and fighting the two of us did, I was never left wondering if my brother loved me.

Smiling for me, he waited until I'd reached the bottom of the stairs before stepping forward. "I see you got your beauty sleep. I'm surprised Victoria wasn't able to con you into going out to lunch with her."

Lunch? Victoria had gone out for lunch? I didn't show my surprise at what he'd just said by so much as a blink. Now I understood a little more why Anya had called. I would have bet good money that my sister had met up with Volkov for her supposed lunch. No wonder Victoria let me sleep. She had wanted some alone time with her wolf.

"Have you seen Ciro?" I changed the subject by asking. "I need to talk to him."

My brother's brows shot toward the roof, but I thought I saw flash of sly amusement in his eyes. "About?"

"None of your damn business, Cristiano," I snapped at him, hating that he had always known about my feelings for his best friend. He'd never teased me about it, but then again, I'd never given him the chance to. "I would like to speak to him. Is he here?"

He shrugged. "Earlier. He left for his mother's about an hour or so ago."

Damn it. Why had I expected it to be easy? "Have a car pulled around for me. I'll just go over and see Mary. I haven't seen her in forever." I loved Ciro's mother. She was sweet and kind and I wasn't completely sure how she'd given birth to such a beast like Ciro. Mary Donati was so tiny compared to her son that it looked impossible for her to be his mother.

My brother sighed, concern darkening his voice when he spoke. "Just be careful, Scarlett."

"I'm always careful," I assured him with a small smile. "Give me ten minutes. I want to say hello to Papa before I go."

Without giving him time to reply, I walked around him and back to my father's office. The door was closed, telling me that he had company, so I tapped on it twice before opening it and sticking my head inside. Since there had been no guards outside, I'd known that whomever was inside was more friend than foe.

My father's head lifted and he offered me a warm smile, but my attention was quickly pulled to the man sitting across from him. Benito Donati was my father's closest and most trusted friend. He looked so much like his son, I could easily picture what Ciro would look like with thirty more years on him, and I had to admit that it would look very, very good on him.

"*Zio* Ben," I stepped fully into the office as both men got to their feet. "It's so good to see you."

Benito chuckled as he opened his arms, and I hugged him. "There's the little ballbreaker," he teased as he pulled back enough to smile down at me. "Beautiful as ever, I see."

"I was just about to go over to see Mary," I told him.

"Good, good." He glanced at my father. "She's a good girl, Vito. How'd a fuckup like you raise such a good girl like her?"

"She's just like her papa, that's how."

I pulled away from Ben to hug my father. "I just wanted to say hello before I went out, Papa."

Papa's arms tightened around me for a moment before he pulled back and tapped my nose twice. "Just be careful, *passerotta.* Stay with your security men. Don't make me worry."

"Yes, Papa." I kissed his cheek, then turned to Benito. "See you later, *Zio* Ben."

The car was already waiting in front of the house with the driver behind the wheel. Another guard held the back door open for me and then climbed into the front passenger side with the driver. Neither asked where I was going but the driver turned straight for the Donatis' home that was several miles away.

Once there, I got out and climbed the steps to the front door. The two men waited by the car, knowing I would be well protected inside the Donatis' house. Both Benito and Ciro made sure that Mary was safe and she rarely left her home without her husband or son to accompany her. Ringing the doorbell, I waited for someone to answer.

When the door opened I'd been expecting to see Mary or even her housekeeper—hell, Ciro even. The woman who stood on the other side of the door was a stranger to me though. She was beautiful, with her obviously dyed cherry-red hair and big blue eyes. She was on the shorter side, but she had a body to die for, compared to mine, which her jeans and tank top only enhanced. Her smile was genuine, but I could see something in her eyes that told me she was assessing me just as much as I was her.

"Can I help you?" she asked after a small pause between the two of us, her curiosity just as strong as my own.

"Is Ciro here?" There was no use pretending I'd come for any other reason but the real one. The need to talk to him had only increased when I'd found out Victoria had gone out. As much as I'd missed Mary, I had to get to the bottom of what Volkov was up to before I could focus on anything else.

Surprise darkened the other woman's eyes for a moment before she hid it. Of all the reasons I could be standing on the other side of the front door, apparently Ciro hadn't been on her list. "I think he might still be here." She stepped back, waving me inside. "Come on in and we'll see. If not, I'm sure Mary can lead you in the right direction."

Was that possessiveness I'd heard in her voice? Jealousy hit me right in the stomach, but I refused to show it as I crossed the threshold. I had no idea who this woman was but from the way she was acting I got the impression she was close to Ciro. Ciro, who got close to no one. Was he involved with her? She was apparently staying under his mother's roof, which meant Mary must have liked her, and Ciro wouldn't introduce his mother to any woman he wasn't serious about.

Pain twisted in my chest as the jealousy ate a hole in my stomach. It made me hate this woman and I didn't even know her name. I had the urge to stab her in the back as she led the way through the huge house to the kitchen. It would have been so easy to kill her and have the two men who had came with me get rid of her body. No one would miss her except for Ciro.

Like I cared.

"Who is it, dear?" I heard Mary call out as we got closer to the kitchen.

"Someone here to see Ciro," the woman in front of me called back before pushing open the kitchen door.

Reining in my urge to kill the stranger in front of me, I put a smile on my face as I stepped into the kitchen. Mary Donati was sitting at the huge island in the middle of her beautiful kitchen, drinking a cup of tea. When she saw me, her face brightened and she jumped to her feet. "Scarlett, what a pleasure."

I let the smaller woman enfold me in her arms, giving me a long, motherly hug that filled my heart like nothing else could. I didn't remember my own mother very well. She'd died when Victoria and I were still toddlers. Mary, however, had always been a part of our lives and had been the one we had turned to when we'd needed advice about female things.

"I was going to give you a few more days to rest up from your trip before I stole you away for some girl time," Mary informed me as she pulled back, her blue eyes so like her son's moving over me with a critical but loving guise. "Where's Victoria?"

I shrugged. "She was already on the move before I got out of bed," I told her as I glanced around the kitchen.

My gaze instantly landed on the big man standing on the other side of the island, a mug of coffee lifted to his lips as he watched me over the rim. Dressed in black dress pants that looked like they had been tailored to fit his narrow hips and toned thighs, with a simple gray T-shirt over his hard chest and the ivy cap he never seemed to be without, he was everything I craved all rolled into one dangerous package.

I forced my eyes away and back to Mary. "I'm sorry, I actually came to talk to Ciro."

Amusement I didn't completely understand filled her eyes. "Ah. Well, then, I won't keep you." She glanced over her shoulder at her son. "Play nicely, you two."

Ciro set his mug down on the counter and deliberately glanced from me to the pretty brunette who was still standing quietly by the kitchen door. I didn't look at her—couldn't look at her. Not if she was looking at him the way I wanted to be able to freely. Affection crossed his face before he could hide it, and my jealousy only doubled. Had Ciro ever looked at me like that? There was such tenderness in his expression that it was like a slap to the face. If he had wanted to hurt me, nothing could have been more affective.

Mary cleared her throat, thankfully pulling my attention back to her and away from the thought of how badly I wanted to destroy the other woman's pretty, pretty face. "Scarlett, I don't believe you've met my niece. This is Felicity. Felicity, this is Vito's eldest daughter, Scarlett."

Niece.

Relief flooded through me, which only pissed me off twice as much. I'd seriously been about to hurt this woman for no other reason that she had the one thing—the *only* thing—I'd ever wanted. Ciro loved her. Now I knew she was his cousin and that the affection I saw between the two was only because they were family.

Would he have told me that she was his cousin, though? If Mary hadn't been there, would he have let me believe he had a closer, more intimate connection to the beautiful Felicity?

I had to stop letting Ciro affect me so strongly, but I honestly had no idea how to turn it off. It hurt in a way I couldn't ever begin to explain.

Felicity stepped forward, her hand already extended. "Hi. It's a pleasure to meet you."

I shook her hand but quickly released it, my feelings too close to the surface for me to care if I was rude or not. "You too," I muttered through gritted teeth. I was still trying to get my head wrapped around the sudden realization that Ciro wasn't involved with her.

"Scarlett and I will talk in the study, Ma," Ciro told his mother.

"Of course." Mary gave me a warm smile, ignoring the fact that I had just snubbed her niece so coldly. The amusement that had been in her eyes earlier had only intensified.

I didn't know what she was laughing about. I saw nothing funny about any of this.

Chapter 7

Ciro

I opened the door to my parents' study and waited for Scarlett to enter before following her inside and closing the door. Her shoulders were stiff, her head held high while her guarded eyes gazed at something on the wall behind my father's desk.

I'd seen the jealousy that had been eating at her as she'd tried not to look at Felicity. For a moment I'd even thought about letting her continue thinking that Felicity was my lover. It had been funny for all of five seconds before I realized that she was hurting.

The thought of Scarlett in any kind of pain, physical or emotional, drove me fucking nuts. If my mother hadn't explained who Felicity was when she had, I would have done it myself. I'd killed men to keep my cousin's identity a secret. It was one of the reasons I was glad she lived on the other side of the country, surrounded by an entire MC that would give their lives for her. But I couldn't keep it from Scarlett.

"I didn't know you had a cousin," she murmured, finally turning to face me.

I'd almost been expecting her to tear into me, but her expression was neutral, her brown eyes almost blank, but that told me more than if she'd started throwing things or yelling. This was her mask, the one she'd been using from the time she was a little girl, the one that she put up when she was hurting or upset to the point that she was already planning someone's painful death. The last time I'd seen that look on her beautiful face, she'd been getting on one of Vito's private jets, heading for Sicily.

I thrust my hands into my pockets to keep from reaching for her. I'd gotten a taste of her skin the night before and like a crack addict I'd been craving more ever since. "It's safer for her not to be linked to me or my father," I explained, and she nodded.

"She's beautiful. You two have the same eyes." She crossed her arms over her chest and pressed her lips together. "I guess I should have figured it out when I saw them."

I just stood there, watching her, aching to touch her. A full minute went by without either of us speaking. She was watching me just as closely as I was watching her. It would have been so easy to reach out, pull her against me and kiss her until neither one of us knew who we were. It would put us both out of our misery.

Fuck, I couldn't even remember the reasons why I shouldn't do just that. It was hard to think when all I wanted was to sink into her wild heat.

"What do you know about Adrian Volkov's personal life?"

The question—that fucker's name coming off her lips—had the force to knock some sense into me. I clenched my hands into fists in my pockets. "Is that what you came here to talk to me about?"

Jealousy hit me right between the eyes, making me see red as I wondered how I would kill Volkov and get rid of his body before nightfall. I'd take my time with him. Cut him up while he screamed over and over again until he passed out from the pain. Then I'd wake his ass up and do it all over again, before tossing his body into a barrel of acid while he was still breathing.

She shrugged, pulling me out of my dark fantasies. "Should I seek you out for any other reason? You've made it pretty plain that you don't want anything to do with me." Her forehead wrinkled and fire blazed in her eyes as she glared up at me. "You had Papa send me away just to get me out of your hair, Ciro."

I didn't need the reminder. It hadn't been Vito's idea to send the twins to live with their grandmother in Sicily. I'd planted it there when Scarlett had made it obvious she had feelings for me. It had been a stupid and desperate idea, but one Vito had taken seriously because he'd known I'd been close to giving in to what I felt for his daughter. I'd told him point blank that I wanted her. Vito hadn't been surprised, but he understood why I didn't think I was good enough for Scarlett. The blood on my hands was mostly there at his orders.

I'd regretted the plan the second she had stepped onto that damn plane. It was in that moment I'd known I was throwing our chance away, but I hadn't made a move to stop her. She deserved so much better than what I could give her. A life where she didn't have to look over her shoulder every minute of the day wondering if one of my enemies was ready to put a blade in her back.

That hadn't stopped me from aching for her, slowly going insane with missing her. For weeks—months—we'd gotten closer and closer. She had become not only the girl I loved, but my best friend.

Now here she stood, more beautiful than I remembered, my need for for having only grown in the time we'd been apart.

How the fuck had I thought I could keep from giving in now?

"Why do you want to know?" I didn't even try to keep the coldness out of my voice. Did she honestly think I would just tell her about Volkov?

"I have my reasons." She shifted on her feet, drawing my eyes to the bare skin of her creamy legs. She had legs for days and I wanted them wrapped around my waist.

Damn it. She knew my fixation for her legs and was trying to distract me to get information.

Forcing my eyes back on her face, I saw the sly little glint in her eyes and knew it was exactly what she was doing. I wanted to wring her little neck, but she knew I wouldn't ever hurt her. Crossing my arms over my chest to mimic her stance, I narrowed my eyes. "What I know about Volkov isn't anything I would ever share with you, Scarlett. He keeps his private life as quiet as I do. So if you wanted to know if he has an opening for a new mistress, then I can't help you. And if you dare to apply for the position, I'll break his fucking neck."

She rolled her eyes at me. "You can be really dense at times, you know that, right?" Shaking her head, she started to move around me to get to the door. "I guess I'll just have to find out about him from someone else. See ya around, Ciro."

As she passed me, I caught her arm and pulled her closer. No way was she going to walk away with that little threat hanging between us. Find out from someone else? Like hell. She'd go looking and get herself in trouble and I'd have to kill some poor fucker.

Her nostrils flared, and I liked the way her eyes dilated when her nose was filled with my cologne. Her next breath shuddered out of her and the pulse at the base of her throat started ticking in time to my own racing heartbeat. "Tell me why you want to know, Scarlett."

Her free hand lifted, pushing at my chest, but her nails unconsciously curled into my shirt. "How many times do I have to tell you I'm not interested in him? I have my reasons for needing to know, Ciro, but not one of them is because I want him for myself. Even though you sent me away..." She stopped, swallowed hard, then boldly met my gaze, knocking the air out of my chest with her next words. "I'm stupid enough to still care about you."

It had taken guts for her to admit that to me, and it wiped away every shred of jealousy I had for Adrian Volkov. I saw her true feelings shining back at me from her brown eyes and knew—fucking knew—that I couldn't keep fighting what we had. I didn't deserve her, but I'd destroy anyone who tried to take her away from me.

First I had to take care of what she'd sought me out for.

"Victoria." There was no other reason she would want to know about the Russian so much. Relief flooded through me and I pulled Scarlett even closer before I could think better of it. Fuck. She smelled good and felt even better. Her body fit against mine perfectly, like she had been made specifically for me.

After only a second of resisting, she came willingly, the top of her head tucking under my chin as she molded her body against mine. I felt the fingertips of her left hand trace over the stubble on my jaw and I closed my eyes, savoring the gentle contact. "I just need to know if there is anything in his personal life that could hurt her," she murmured with a little sigh that made my dick throb.

This was the Scarlett only I'd ever seen. The softer side of her that she kept hidden from everyone, including herself at times. She was so strong—and, fuck, more than a little bitchy—at times that it was impossible for others to see the vulnerable side of her. Before I'd had Vito send her away, she hadn't been afraid to let me see her weaknesses, had known that I would protect her to my last breath. This moment was just a taste of what I'd given up when she'd gone to Sicily.

One minute, I promised myself as I let my hands roam freely down her spine. One minute of touching her was all I would allow myself, and then I would let her go and find out whatever the hell she wanted about Volkov. One single minute of paradise and I'd gladly take an eternity in hell for her.

I was slowly counting down the seconds, savoring each one of them as she let me hold her. A sharp tap on the door was quickly followed by it opening, interrupting us before I'd reached fifty.

I reluctantly released Scarlett as Jet Hannigan stuck his head into the room. The biker was a huge motherfucker and an ex-con, but there were few men I trusted as much as him. Green eyes roamed over the room until they landed first on Scarlett and then me. The shock didn't show on his face, but I could tell by the set of his shoulders that he hadn't been expecting to find her with me.

"Sorry, man. Your mom didn't say you had company."

I shot a glance at Scarlett, saw that her mask was firmly back in place again and then gave the other man my attention. "Scarlett had something for me to handle for her. Let me walk her out and then we can talk."

Jet gave a single firm nod and stepped back as I crossed to the door. Scarlett followed. She kept her hands at her sides and a bored look on her face, but I could still see the pulse beating like a little jackhammer at the base of her throat. It was just as hard for her to turn off what she felt as it was for me, and I was fucking tired of turning it off.

She was quiet as I walked her to the front door. I opened it and waited for her to step outside, but she paused on the threshold, her brown eyes full of curiosity. "Are you really going to find out about Volkov for me?"

"If I don't will you go looking for the answers yourself?" Her silence was the only answer I needed. She would do whatever she had to as long as she found out what she needed about the Russian. She wanted to protect Victoria, and I wanted to protect *her*. "I'll see what I can find out and let you know as soon as I have anything that might upset your sister."

"Thank you, Ciro." Her voice was little more than a whisper as she reached up and pressed her lips to my cheek. I had to clench my hands into fists to keep from grabbing hold of her and never letting go. Not yet. I'd find out about Volkov first, then give in to what we both wanted—fucking needed—so desperately. The feel of her soft, warm lips against my cheek barely lasted a second before she was stepping back and turning away.

I watched as she walked down the steps and let one of her guards open the back door to one of Vito's Town Cars. Once she was inside, the guard lifted his chin in acknowledgement before taking the front passenger seat. As the car pulled away, I slammed the door shut, my body throbbing and my chest squeezing as the only person in the world I couldn't live without rode away.

Chapter 8

Scarlett

My fingers were still shaking as I sat in the back of the Town Car on the drive home. Had that been what I'd gone there wanting? Rather than expecting him to *give* me answers, had I wanted him to *find* them for me?

More to the point, had I been wanting the all-too-brief moment we'd had before the rough-looking guy in the leather vest had interrupted?

Even as the question whispered in the back of my head, I knew what the answer was. Yes, I'd wanted it. Yes, I'd hoped. Yes, I was stupid for not being able to move on. Hell, I was a masochist where Ciro Donati was concerned.

My phone started ringing but I didn't hear it until the guard in the passenger seat glanced back at me. Clenching my hands into fists to stop them from trembling, I finally pulled out my phone. Seeing that it was my sister, I nearly groaned. I might have been able to hide what I was feeling from the men in the front seat, but there wasn't any way I could do it with my twin. She would know the second I answered that I my emotions were too close to the surface.

Grimacing, I reluctantly lifted it to my ear. "Where are you?" I demanded, going on the offensive to distract her from what I was feeling.

"Do I really need to tell you where I am?" She giggled, and I grimaced again, this time for an entirely different reason.

After the night before, I should have realized that Victoria was so into Adrian that she wouldn't even think about what I was doing. I was both relieved that I didn't have to explain myself to her and nervous because there was no telling what Ciro would find out about Volkov. The happiness that was practically radiating through the phone hit me with a blast of real fear for my sister's wellbeing.

Maybe I needed to pull her back a little. Waiting for the answers might do more harm than trying to step in before I had them. "Tor…"

"Uh-oh." She giggled again. "There's that mother-knows-best tone I've been dreading. Chill out, I just had lunch with him. What's the harm in that?"

"Just lunch?" She couldn't really fall in love with the guy over a meal, I assured myself.

No, she had probably been halfway there the night before. "Where are you?" I asked again. "I'll meet you and we can talk."

"I'm on my way home, but I'll have the guys stop and we can have coffee."

"Wait…" I lowered my voice. "Did you just leave?" I glanced at the thin, platinum watch on my left wrist. "Tor, how fucking long were you with him?"

"A while," she hedged, and I nearly groaned again.

"Was eating the only thing that went on?" I heard her giggle again and nearly face-palmed myself at the dirty little way my sister had just taken my question. Holy Christ. My innocent little twin was thinking dirty thoughts. Something more than having a simple meal had taken place.

"Just get home, Victoria," I snapped, worry for her rolling through me and making my stomach clench with anxiety. "We have to talk."

The giggles abruptly stopped. "What's going on, Scarlett?" She sounded unsure now, and I knew I was going to hurt her before Ciro could even get me answers.

I blew out a frustrated breath through my nose. "I'll be home in five minutes. Come up to my room when you get there. Okay?"

"Okay," she whispered, her tone so soft I barely heard her.

I hung up before I said more. What I needed to tell her wasn't something I wanted to do in front of two of my father's men. Their loyalty was to him, not me or Victoria, and I knew they would take whatever information I had straight to him or Cristiano.

We were a few miles away still when the driver pulled to a stop at a red light. I barely remembered his or the other guy's names. They hadn't said more than a hundred words to me in my entire life. Keeping me safe was their only priority, plain and simple.

While we waited for the light to turn green, I glanced out the window, worrying about Victoria. If Adrian was messing with her, playing with her heart to possibly get back at my father, I would destroy him. I wouldn't need Ciro's help to do it, either.

An expensive sports car pulled to a stop beside the Town Car. The driver's window was down, pulling me from the dark thoughts of how I would slit Volkov from neck to navel with the little daggers I'd gotten in Sicily. They were small, sharp and very deadly. I'd been playing with them since I'd bought them, throwing them at targets in my room. I was getting good at hitting the bulls-eye, but I thought I would enjoy tearing the Russian's skin from his flesh with them more.

The driver of the other car had a nice golden complexion, the glasses on his handsome face hiding his eyes from me. I knew he couldn't see me through the tint of the back window, but he was looking right at me, a smug little smile on his face. It was unsettling, but I didn't look away from the man. I guessed him to be in his late twenties, maybe slightly older than my brother and Ciro, but there was a tilt to his chin that was more arrogant than actually confident, unlike the other two men.

From the front seat I heard the guard in the passenger seat mutter a harsh curse. In the next second the car was jerking forward. Before the light had even turned green we were flying through the intersection and headed toward the compound at triple the legal speed.

The guard in the passenger seat pulled out his phone, barking orders so fast I couldn't understand everything he was saying. The gates were already open and as soon as we pulled through, they were quickly closed.

Cristiano was already standing by the steps to the house, his eyes not on the Town Car but at the gate in the distance. I hadn't had time to react to what had just happened, but as I followed my brother's gaze I saw the sports car that had been at the red light and realized that whoever that cocky bastard was, he was bad news.

The guards jumped out before I could even think about moving. The back door opened and Cristiano was there to pull me out. He wrapped his arm around my shoulder, pulling me close to his side, and rushed me into the house.

"Who was that?"

Cristiano slammed the door shut behind us. "Trouble," he growled. "That's Carlo Santino, Jr." His face twisted with rage as he spoke the name.

I knew enough about my father's connections to remember that the Santino family was a West Coast rival. Santino Senior had been trying to push his way into my father's business not only in New York but also in Chicago for decades.

My father and Benito appeared as if out of thin air. I hadn't really thought about the danger of the situation until Papa wrapped his arms around me, muttering curses at Cristiano, and I actually felt him trembling. My father never reacted like this unless he thought something had happened to me or Victoria. That he was now had my heart pounding as I remembered the look on who I assumed was Carlo Jr.'s face.

How had that asshat known where I was? Was he following me?

It wasn't often that something as little as a guy's smile could unsettle me, but right then a shiver went down my spine and all I could think about was how much I wanted Ciro to be the one holding me right then. I knew my father would protect me to his dying breath, but I felt the safest when I was with Ciro.

As if I'd conjured him with that silent plea for him, the door opened and the beast of a man stormed into the house, rage seeming to flood off him in waves. The few guards who had been in the foyer with us suddenly found other things to do.

Papa released me as Ciro stepped forward, but he didn't hold me like I'd wanted. Instead, he just stood there, his blue eyes stormy as he clenched his hands into fists at his sides. "Did he speak to you?"

I shook my head. "No. He just stopped at the red light and looked straight at me."

He turned away, his shoulders so tense I thought he might punch something. "Don't leave the damn house," he ordered as he opened the door again. "Make sure Victoria stays close too."

I felt winded as he left, my heart racing as I thought about Victoria possibly being in danger from that little creep.

"Where is Victoria?" Papa suddenly demanded.

“She’s on her way home, Papa,” I assured him, hoping to distract him before he could ask who she was with. “I spoke to her before everything happened.”

“You girls are not to leave the compound again until we get Santino under control,” Cristiano grumbled. “It’s too dangerous for you with that bastard running around.”

I wanted to roll my eyes at my brother, but stopped myself before I could. Even though I was a little shaken now, I wasn’t scared of Santino Jr. Ciro would deal with him, I was sure of it. Whatever Santino was up to he wouldn’t last long now that he’d pissed that particular *capo* off.

Chapter 9

Ciro

Blood was still pounding in my ears as I jumped into the back of the SUV I'd told Desi to keep running when I'd gone into Vito's house. I shouldn't have taken the time to stop, but I'd needed to see for myself that Scarlett was safe and unharmed. She hadn't even been shaken by the whole incident, while I'd been trembling so bad that I was scared I would have crushed her if I'd dared to touch her.

I couldn't believe the balls Jr had. That fucker must have been watching her from the time she'd left the compound. He had a death wish, that was more than obvious, and I was going to give him exactly what he wanted as soon as I got my hands on that little prick.

"She okay?"

I didn't even glance at Jet Hannigan, who had been waiting for me with my men. He hadn't hesitated to jump into the situation with me when

Cristiano had called to tell me what Jr had done. The Hannigan brothers had more reasons than I did to want to get their hands on the bastard, but now that he'd approached Scarlett, I wasn't just going to hand him over to the MC. Not alive.

"It would take more than this to disturb Scarlett," I muttered as Desi pulled into traffic.

I wasn't looking at the biker, but I could hear the grin in his voice when he spoke. "She's got some balls on her, that's for sure. Interesting female you have there, man."

"She's not mine," I bit out. Not yet, anyway. I wasn't about to announce that to anyone, however, least of all the ex-con who was involved with my little cousin or my two men who were watching me with unreadable eyes.

"He's in the wind again, *capo*," Paco informed me from the front passenger seat. "We lost him when we stopped."

Fuck. I knew better than to pause, but I would have lost my mind if I hadn't checked on Scarlett. "I want every available man looking for that motherfucker." I spared Jet a glance. "Including your guys."

He shrugged. "Colt and Raider are already out with four of your men. I'll tell Uncle Jack and Trigger to get out in the field as well."

"You too." I had growled the command. The MC guys might have been there for their own reasons, but they still worked for Vito and took their orders straight from me. "You know Jr as well as I do. Put that brain of yours to good use, Hannigan. I want that fucker found tonight."

The biker didn't even blink at my harsh tone. We'd been working together for years and I doubted he was as scared of me as my own men were, but he wasn't stupid either. He knew I wouldn't hesitate to put a bullet in his head. "I'm on it, Ciro."

I reined in my anger, hating that I'd let my guard down. This was one of the reasons I didn't want to get involved with Scarlett. Where she was concerned, my guard was down and my emotions were too involved to treat the situation with the cold-mindedness that it needed.

"We'll find him, *capo*," Desi assured me from the driver seat.

I clenched my jaw and nodded but didn't speak as the man drove us into the city. Jr had better enjoy breathing while he still could. He was a walking corpse as far as I was concerned.

Scarlett

I watched Victoria as she paced back and forth in her bedroom. I'd told her about my call with Anya and then everything that had followed. She, like me, wasn't concerned about the whole Santino issue. After twenty-one years of having to deal with enemies like him, we knew the idiot couldn't touch us, and even if he tried, Ciro and Cristiano would handle it.

Her focus was on Volkov right then.

"What does that even mean?" she kept muttering to herself. My happy sister was getting angrier by the minute. Angry at Anya. At Adrian. Herself. "Why would she be so vague like that?" She stopped in front of me. The hurt I saw shining back at me made me glad I'd changed my mind and told her now rather than later. "Am I not good enough for her brother, Scarlett? Is that it? Or is there really something he's keeping from me?"

I didn't know the answer to any of those questions and it pissed me off that I couldn't give them to her and offer her peace of mind. "You're plenty good enough for the likes of Volkov, Tor. Any man would be blessed to have you look twice at him. Look, Ciro is looking into it for me, but maybe..." She had started to turn away but her head snapped back around.

"Maybe what?"

"Maybe you should just come out and ask him about it. Maybe he'll tell you the truth, maybe he won't. But wouldn't you rather speak to him about this than let it eat at you?" Her chin trembled and I reached for her hands, pulling her down beside me on the bed.

"I'm scared to know the answer, Scarlett," she whispered. "I like him, really like him. I thought the feelings were mutual when we had lunch today." A blush filled her cheeks, making me wonder if my earlier guess that something else had happened today besides the sharing of a meal was true.

"Tor, did you sleep with him?" I felt her pulse jump under my fingers where I was still holding her wrist, and knew I had my answer.

"We didn't have sex, but…" She shrugged and turned her head away, avoiding my gaze. "Our first kiss got carried away. Things happened."

I wasn't about to lecture my sister. She was an adult and could do what she wanted with who she wanted. But was Volkov free to do those things with her? That was the million-dollar question. I picked up her phone and went through her call log. The last one she'd made was a number I didn't recognize, and I knew it had to belong to the Russian. Why she hadn't added him to her contacts I had no clue, but it didn't matter right then.

Swiping my thumb over the number, I hit the speaker button and waited. It took eight rings before he answered. "I'm busy at the moment, *kotyonok*." His deep voice was low, but his tone was gentle. "Can I call you back?"

"I need to talk to you," Victoria told him, but she hadn't yet gotten her emotions under control and he picked up on the small catch in her voice as easily as if he had been the one sitting next to her instead of me.

"What's wrong?" he demanded, all gentleness gone from his voice now. "Did you make it home safely?"

Even to my ears he sounded concerned and more than a little possessively overprotective. That had to mean something, damn it, and I hoped that it was all a big mistake. I wanted Victoria and Adrian to have a chance together.

If he wasn't some scumbag who was playing my sister.

"I'm fine," she murmured, trying harder to keep her voice even but was unsuccessful. "I just thought I owed it to you to let you know I won't be seeing you again, Adrian."

There was a long pause on his end and I could actually feel the tension coming off the man even through the phone. "Why?" he bit out, his tone more menacing than any I'd ever heard before. Considering how Ciro had reacted earlier, that was saying a hell of a lot.

She met my eyes, searching for an answer. I didn't have one to give her because when I'd told her to talk to him this hadn't exactly been what I was expecting her to say. I'd told her to ask him, not dump him on the spot.

"Victoria, I asked you why," Volkov repeated, his tone not as harsh this time, as if he could feel her hesitation. "*Kotyonok,* what's the matter? Talk to me, little one. I can't fix this if I don't know what's hurt you."

She swallowed hard. "Someone close to me has shown me that a future with you is impossible." She whispered but she might as well have screamed it at him from the static-filled silence that followed. She bit her lip briefly to keep it from trembling, but quickly continued. "You're not free to be with me, are you, Adrian?"

"Who told you?" he demanded with a ferocity that had my twin lose the battle with her tears and trembling chin. "Tell me who told you these things, *kotyonok*. Now."

She swallowed her sob as the tears fell freely. "It doesn't matter who. All that matters is that it's the truth. I thought we had something special, but obviously I was only being stupid. I don't play those kinds of games, Adrian and I'll never settle for being anyone's second choice. It was nice knowing you, but it's over now. G-goodbye."

"Victoria!" He roared her name, but she was already disconnecting. With trembling fingers, she turned the phone off and then fell against my chest, her sobs so intense that they shook my own body. She wasn't the type to have a passing infatuation. When she loved, she went all in, and sadly she'd been in over her head with Volkov.

I swallowed my anger, knowing my sister needed a loving shoulder to cry on right then. How could that bastard do this? Victoria was special and he'd apparently only been playing with her. I'd hoped it was just a bunch of hot air being blown by Anya, but obviously she'd only been watching out for my sister. I guess I owed her a thank you, because it wasn't likely that Victoria would have found out until it was too late otherwise.

If it wasn't already.

With each tear she cried, each sob that seemed to rip her apart, I wanted to chop Volkov into tiny little pieces. Maybe send them to the woman he was already involved with along with a note telling her to watch out for cheating bastards in the future. I kept those thoughts to myself, though, as I stroked Victoria's hair like I'd always done when she was upset.

Chapter 10

Ciro

The lights flashing in the club irritated the hell out of my yes, but I didn't blink as I watched Anya Volkov across the bar top on the second floor of her club. The music was loud enough to make a person deaf if they spent too much time in there, but I could practically hear her nails tapping on the smooth surface. The little Russian beauty gave me a bored roll of her eyes and I had to grit my teeth to keep from grabbing her by the neck and demand answers.

Since I couldn't find Jr, I figured I'd start on finding the answers Scarlett was so set on discovering. I knew so little about Volkov's personal life I'd started at the first place I did know he had connections with. Anya was a little hardass and she ran her business exactly the way the club was named, with an iron hand. I'd had to deal with her a few times over the last few years, but more often than not it was Cristiano who dealt with her.

The place was full even though it wasn't the busiest night of the week, and her staff was running around on both floors getting things done. Anya just stood there, glaring at me with a darkness I could easily see matched that of her soul. "I don't know what you're talking about. I haven't spoken to Scarlett since she and her sister were in here the other night."

She was the perfect liar, and if anyone else but Scarlett had told me about the phone call she had gotten the day before, I might have even believed Anya. I picked up the shot of vodka she had poured for me and tossed it back. Setting the glass back on the bar top, I watched her with dispassionate eyes.

The longer I stared at her, the colder her eyes grew. "Why do you even care?" she snapped. "Victoria broke off whatever it was that was going on with my brother yesterday. So it shouldn't matter."

I shrugged. "To some, maybe."

She put her hands on the smooth, clean surface of the bar top and leaned toward me, her face a mask of cold anger as she met my gaze without flinching. "Stay out of it, Donati."

"It must be something ugly if you're so set on keeping it a secret, Anya." I lifted a curious brow at her when her eyes shifted and I realized it was a tell. Interesting. "A wife?" She moved back before I could see if her gaze shifted.

"Fuck off, Ciro. You're stinking up my club."

I pulled out a few bills from my pocket and tossed them at her. "Thanks for the drink. I'll be seeing you around, Anya."

She took the cash and threw it back in my face before flipping me off. "Go to hell."

Her fierceness actually had a small grin tugging at the corners of my lips. "I'll be sure and save you a seat." Leaving the cash where it had landed, I turned and walked away, knowing I risked a knife in the back for turning my back on the little tyrant.

Desi and Paco were waiting for me at the bottom of the stairs where I'd left them with the two bouncers. Neither of them spoke to me until we were back in the SUV parked behind the club. "Paco, Vito has someone watching Volkov, but I want you to keep an eye on him as well. Anya too." I had all my men looking for Jr, but I could spare one to check the Russian out.

"On it, *capo*."

"Desi, get me another background check on him. This time go all the way back to before he was in prison in Moscow." Desi was just as deadly with a computer as he was with a gun.

"Got it." Desi pulled the vehicle into traffic. "You want us to drop you at home or the compound?"

I hadn't been to my own place in days, not since before Scarlett had gotten home. The idea of being in my bed, when she was in her own, held little appeal to me. "Compound," I muttered.

Without a word, he headed for the Vitucci compound. While he drove, I sent out texts to all my men, wanting reports of their progress at locating Jr so far. No one had any updates, and that set my teeth on edge. The motherfucker was playing with me and I'd never been one for games.

By the time I was finished, the gates at the compound were being opened. Pocketing my phone, I jumped out of the back of the SUV and climbed the steps to the front door while Desi and Paco went home. Inside, the place was quiet. It was after midnight, so I'd expected most of the household to be in bed. There were still plenty of guards patrolling the house though.

Pulling off my ivy cap, I climbed the stairs to the second floor, but I didn't go to the room that had become mine over the years. I stopped outside of Scarlett's bedroom. I hadn't seen her since the day before. I'd spent the night before checking out possible places Jr might think to hide out in, but had come up empty-handed. I was going on forty-two hours without sleep. My body should have been demanding some down time, but all I needed was to make sure Scarlett was okay.

Thinking that she was asleep, I carefully cracked open her door and stepped inside. The only light to see by was that of the television that was on mute, casting a soft glow over her bed. Quietly closing the door behind me, I crossed to her. Her head was on her pillow, the covers pulled up to her chest. One arm was tucked under her head, the other lying across her flat stomach. The light from the TV made her skin glow, enticing me to come closer. She looked like an angel.

Standing over her, I let my eyes trace over every inch of her beautiful face. Just looking at her made my dick hard. I ached to climb in beside her and memorize every inch of her body.

"Ciro." She murmured my name and her eyes opened before I could even move. I wasn't sure I even wanted to. Lifting a hand, she pushed a few strands of her hair back from her face. "What's wrong?"

"Nothing." How could anything be wrong when I was there with the only person who mattered?

Her brow furrowed. "Then why are you here?"

I sat down on the edge of her bed. "There's no other place I wanted to be," I told her honestly and watched as her eyes widened before she could mask her reaction. "Tell me to go if you don't want me here, Scarlett."

For the longest time she just continued to lay there, staring up at me. I couldn't read her expression, but the way she was watching me had my dick thickening even more. Instead of telling me to go, she slid over in bed and pulled the covers back. "Sleep with me?" she offered in a voice barely above a whisper.

I knew I shouldn't, but the enticement was too strong to resist. Tossing my cap on the floor I kicked off my shoes and pulled my belt free from my pants. I didn't dare take off anything else. The temptation was already at dangerous levels and I knew I wouldn't fight my need if I took off my shirt or pants.

Emptying my pockets, I placed my gun on the nightstand and then climbed into bed beside her. It was a king, offering us both plenty of room, but as soon as my head hit the pillow I pulled her against me. She came willingly, her breath leaving her on a little sigh as she pillowed her head on my chest and dropped her arm over my stomach.

The room was chilly, just the way she liked to keep it, and I pulled the covers up over us. This was pure bliss. I hadn't ever experienced it before until right at that moment. With her slight weight against me, her warmth seeping into mine, I began to relax despite the ache in my dick. She shifted, finding a more comfortable position, and in the next moment she was asleep again.

I pressed my lips to the top of her head, breathing in the sweet floral scent of her shampoo. My muscles started to feel heavy and I let sleep take me too.

***

If falling asleep with Scarlett was bliss, waking up with her still tucked against me like she belonged there was pure hell. My entire body was throbbing with the need to roll her onto her back and slide between her thighs.

She shifted in her sleep, one leg sliding against mine before wrapping it over both of them. A small little mewling sound in pleasure and she rubbed her hand up my chest. I bit back a groan and told myself to get the hell out of there before I did something stupid, but she cuddled closer and I was helpless to move for fear of waking her. She was comfortable, and if it weren't for the raging hard-on I had right then, I would have been too.

I heard my phone vibrating on the nightstand and shot it an irritated glance. My eyes fell on the clock beside my phone and gun and I nearly groaned again. 9:08. Hell, I hadn't slept past six since I was a teenager. I was usually up and taking care of business by now. My men were probably wondering if I was dead.

I hated leaving her, but there were things that needed my attention. Carefully, I untangled her and slid out from under her. As I stood, already putting my gun back in place, she yawned. "Don't go," she implored, still half asleep.

I bent and pressed a kiss to her forehead. "I have work to do, baby."

Her bottom lip pouted out and my heart nearly stopped at the sight of her like that. Her red hair wild and sleep tousled spread out across her pillow, her face pink with sleep as she looked up at me through her lashes and that plump bottom lip practically begging me to suck on it. "Will you come back tonight?"

I traced my thumb down her jaw and across that lip I wanted to taste so fucking bad. "I'll come back," I promised. "Stay out of trouble today, yeah?"

A smile teased at her lips, but she didn't answer. Instead she pulled the pillow I'd used to her chest and closed her eyes, sleep already overtaking her once more. Hell. The urge to blow off my responsibilities and climb back in next to her was almost too hard to fight, but my phone started vibrating again. Cursing under my breath, I picked it up and waited until I was out of the room before answering.

"What?" I growled as I headed for the stairs.

"Would you be interested in knowing that Cristiano just went into Volkov's apartment building?" Paco asked, uncertainty in his voice.

"Did he see you?" As far as I knew Cristiano had no business even being in that part of the city. I knew that Anya had an apartment in the building, but Adrian had the entire top floor for himself. He might not have even been there to see either one of them. Either way, Cristiano was a big boy and didn't need me to babysit his ass.

I just didn't want him to know yet that I was interested in Volkov, and more to the point, why. I loved Cristiano like a brother, but not even for him would I break Scarlett's confidence. She'd come to me, had trusted me more than anyone else, and I wasn't about to give her a reason to regret that trust.

"No, *capo*. Just didn't know if that was something you wanted me to report or not."

I scrubbed a hand over my face. What Cristiano did was none of my business, unless it put Scarlett at risk. He could take care of himself. "Keep that information between us, Paco, and keep an eye on Anya and her brother. I want to know who comes and goes. Get any names to Desi so he can check them out."

"On it."

Chapter 11

Scarlett

"I saw something really intriguing yesterday." I was only playing with my lunch as I sat in the dining room with my father. It was the first real meal we'd had together, but food held little appeal for me.

I put the blame on Ciro.

He'd promised he'd come back the night before and he hadn't. There had been no text, no call to say why he hadn't come back to the compound and let me use him as a human pillow. It was like I'd been pushed out of his mind the second my door had shut behind him. I didn't know if I was more hurt or angry.

Refusing to let either emotion show on my face, I gave Papa my full attention. "What was it, Papa?"

His brown eyes were almost assessing as he skimmed them over my face for a moment. But there was nothing in his voice that prepared me for the next words out of his mouth. "I saw Ciro leaving your room with his shoes in his hand yesterday morning. Care to comment?"

Hell.

Before I'd gone to Sicily…

No, I was done pretending. Before Papa had sent me away at Ciro's request, I'd made no secret about how I felt for Ciro. There had been no use in pretending I was anything but in love with him. For a few short weeks I'd thought we were getting closer and that it was only a matter of time before he approached my father about it. I'd never dreamed that he would ask him to send me and Victoria away.

Papa had known exactly how I felt, and I could only assume he'd known about Ciro's feelings as well, but he'd never voiced his opinion on it. Not until I'd been put on a plane for another fucking country. To me, that had more or less been Papa saying he didn't approve, which had gutted me. I'd still been in shock when I first got to Sicily, but it quickly became apparent that I'd only imagined how Ciro felt about me. I'd come home thinking I was ready to move on, that I could get over him and find someone else to fall for. It had been three damn years, for Christ's sake.

Wrong.

I wasn't ready, not by a long shot.

As for Ciro, he was making my head spin. He practically roared 'stay away' only to turn around and pull me close. Now I knew that I hadn't been wrong when I thought he felt the same way as I did. He was just fighting it.

I wasn't sure if fighting his feelings was worse than making me think he didn't care at all.

"Nothing happened," I assured my father, because I wasn't sure what he was fishing around for. If he'd been too upset about finding Ciro leaving my room like that, he would have put a bullet in the back of Ciro's head then and there.

Vito shrugged. "I wasn't concerned that something had. My concern was for you and the obvious lack of appeal your food currently holds for you, *passerotta*. I don't like seeing you like this."

"I'm fine, Papa."

He easily saw through my lie. "The Scarlett I know and love more than life itself wouldn't just sit there and let a guy fuck with her head. She'd be out there busting his balls until he either got his head out of his ass or left the country. Don't let Ciro play with your heart this time around, *passerotta*. I love that boy, but if he breaks your heart again I won't hesitate to take care of him personally."

Take care of him personally?

That thought was enough to push all my wrong buttons.

I pushed my chair back from the table. "Let's be honest here, Papa. You *let* him break my heart." His eyes widened in surprise and I glared at him. I loved my father dearly, but I'd let his part in what had happened slide for long enough. "You sent me away. You knew I loved him and yet you put me on a fucking plane instead of letting me 'bust his balls or make him leave the country,' as you put it just now."

Tossing my napkin on the table, I stood. "It took me over a year to forgive you for that, Papa. I think I might have forgiven Ciro too, because I was way too young to know how I really felt back then. Coming home has shown me that much at least."

"Scarlett—"

"Excuse me, Papa, I'm not very hungry," I told him as I left the room, ignoring his appeal for me to stop.

As I left the dining room, the front door opened and in walked the reason for all my problems. Ciro entered the foyer and stopped in his tracks when he saw me walking toward him. Something in his blue eyes darkened as I stepped past him without so much as a word in greeting, and started up the stairs.

After the conversation I'd had with my father, I didn't have the energy to deal with him right then. I was going on only a few hours of sleep because I'd waited up most of the night for him. It was nice to see that he wasn't dead, at least, although that had been at the very bottom of my list of possible things that had kept him from keeping his promise to come back. I was pretty sure Death was just as scared of Ciro Donati as any other man was.

"I have the information you wanted." He spoke quietly, but his words still had me stopping halfway up the stairs.

Schooling my face to show nothing of the maelstrom of emotions swirling around inside of me, I turned to face him.

He took the stairs two at a time, stopping when we were on an even eye level. "You have dark circles under your eyes, Scarlett."

I shrugged. "Who cares? What did you find out?"

"Volkov is married."

My stomach bottomed out at that news, knowing how destroyed Victoria would be. She had played a good game the day she'd broken it off with Adrian, but I'd seen the way she'd kept looking at her phone the day before. How she would jump every time it would so much as buzz.

"You're sure?" I had to know that this was credible information before I told my sister.

"I had one of my men keep an eye on both Adrian and his sister. Everyone who entered and left their apartment building was checked out, Scarlett. I questioned the woman myself last night."

"I bet you did," I muttered under my breath, but he had the hearing of a predator and easily heard me.

"What the hell does that mean?" he said with a growl.

"Nothing," I snapped and turned to finish climbing the stairs. "Thanks for the help, Ciro. I appreciate it."

"That's it?" he called after me. "Your thank you feels more like a fuck you, Scarlett."

"Probably because it is. See you around, Ciro."

"What the hell just happened?" I heard him mutter to himself, but I kept going.

I was done chasing him. Done going to him for help. Done putting myself out there for him to stomp on my heart because he was too much of a pussy to take what I could give him. Done, period.

If he wanted me, then he had to be the one to do the chasing.

Upstairs, I paused outside of Victoria's door. I knew she was in there, that she'd been more or less hiding since she'd made that call to Volkov. It had hurt her then, but I was sure she hadn't taken it nearly as seriously as she had put on. I didn't know what was going on with her. Part of me suspected that she was even still talking to the Russian.

Now that I knew what Anya had been warning me against, I knew I was about to destroy my sister.

Clenching my jaw, I prepared myself for what was about to happen, and knocked on her door.

"Just a sec," she called.

Yeah, she was definitely hiding something. If I'd just walked in like I normally would have, I knew I probably would have caught her on the phone with him, or texting.

Moments later, the door opened and Victoria stood there looking rumpled. Her cheeks were pink, her eyes sparkling with a banked excitement I knew I was going to completely snuff out before this was over.

"What's wrong?" she demanded when she saw it was me. "You look like you want to kill someone."

"I do," I muttered. "I have to talk to you. Can I come in?"

Her entire face seemed to fall. "What did you find out?" she whispered.

I glanced behind me, saw a guard doing his hourly rounds, and then pushed her back into the bedroom. Shutting the door and locking it so that Cristiano or anyone else couldn't walk in on us, I took her arm and pulled her over to the bed. Pushing her onto the end of it, I crouched down in front of her, holding her hands that seemed to grow colder by the second.

"You've been talking to him, haven't you, Tor?" If anyone but me had asked the question I knew she could have kept the perfect poker face and told a bald-faced lie. Instead I watched as pink filled her cheeks and she glanced away, unable to meet my eyes. That was the only answer I needed. "So he didn't explain to you that he's a married man?"

Brown eyes identical to my own snapped back to my face and I watched as every drop of blood seemed to seep from her skin, leaving her as pale as a ghost. "No, he's not," she whispered. "He can't be."

"I'm so sorry, Tor, but he is." I tightened my hold on her hands when they started to tremble. "Ciro wouldn't lie about something like that. He talked to Volkov's wife personally last night."

"No." She shook her head and jerked her hands away before standing. Crossing to the window, she glared sightlessly out into the sun-filled back yard. "No!"

I didn't speak, knowing she didn't need me to do anything but be there when she finally let herself believe the truth.

She stood there for more than ten minutes, her anger seeming to fill every inch of the room. This

Victoria was dangerous and I almost pitied Volkov for what she would do to him in the end. Almost.

Turning from the window, she wrapped her arms around herself, almost as if she were trying to hold it close so that her anger wouldn't turn into the pain I saw darkening her eyes.

"Who is she?"

"I didn't ask, because I knew I would tell you if I did," I told her honestly. "His wife isn't your enemy, Tor. He is. He played you, and if you have still been talking to him, knowing that he had a secret like this—"

"He told me it was a mistake," she bit out between gritted teeth. "A mistake. Right. I'm so fucking stupid. And naïve. How did I let some guy make me that gullible, Scarlett?"

"Because you fell for him and women do stupid, naïve things when they're in love," I told her point-blank and watched as she flinched but didn't deny it. She loved him, and once the anger passed she would be shattered.

Chapter 12

Scarlett

"Well, this place looks fun." I tried to smile for my sister, but she only gave me an uninterested nod of her head as she looked around the crowded club.

It had been my idea to sneak out for a little fun. I hadn't been able to watch my sister fall into a deeper depression a second longer and had hoped that a little time in a club dancing and letting guys drool over her would cheer her up. Instead it had only made her sulkier.

If this was what it felt like to deal with my moodiness, then I was sincerely sorry for every time I'd acted this way. I hated seeing my normally sunshine-happy sister being swallowed up by the darkness of a broken heart.

"Let's get a drink," I urged as I took her elbow and practically dragged her over to the bar. "We need a buzz going on."

I wanted more than a buzz so I could forget about my own aching heart, but knew I needed to keep a clear head to watch out for Victoria. I hadn't seen Ciro in days. I'd stuck to my new decision to keep away from him and make him come to me if I was really what he wanted. No more chasing, no more putting my heart out there for him to walk all over.

He hadn't come looking for me. Hadn't tried to call. It was like I was an afterthought and that hurt. Bad. My anger was all gone now, the only thing left was a big bruise on my cracked heart and I hated that he could make me feel so damaged. I'd thought a night out would do not only my sister good, but me as well.

After two shots of tequila each, I pulled her out onto the dance floor. Of the two of us, Victoria was definitely the better dancer, but I still enjoyed it. When I was dancing, I let go of everything that felt like it was weighing me down and just let the music lead me. It was kind of cathartic and peaceful, even when surrounded by hundreds of strangers.

It took a few songs, but Victoria started to loosen up enough to enjoy dancing with me. Guys came up to us several times, but I sent them packing before they could even open their mouths. If anyone tried to get between us, I pretended to be drunk and 'accidently' clipped them in the balls. After the second guy got nut-punched no one else was brave enough to so much as approach us.

That at least had my twin smiling, but only for a few minutes. Her phone buzzed from time to time and I knew it was Adrian, with the way her brown eyes actually had flames in them. The flames quickly died down each time when her phone would stop and her voicemail alert would make her phone vibrate. Her inbox must have been overflowing by now because she hadn't listened to any of them.

She hadn't shared with me how she'd broken it off with Volkov after I'd told her about his wife, but I knew she'd locked herself in her room for twelve hours and I'd had to get one of Papa's guards to pick the lock so I could get in to check on her and make sure her blood sugar was at a safe level. It hadn't been and I'd had to force-feed her juice and a sandwich.

I'd been terrified for my sister because she had acted like she had wanted to die. She wouldn't talk to me and if I wasn't there to keep an eye on her I knew she would just let her diabetes win.

Adrian had a lot to answer for. The next time I saw him, I was going to end his miserable existence.

After an hour of dancing, I had to use the bathroom. I took Victoria back to the bar to hydrate and told her I'd be right back. She was looking miserable once again and I figured it was time to go. The club was crowded so it was a workout just to get to the bathrooms. Two women a little older than me came out of the bathroom as I reached for the door, both of them stumbling drunkenly and giggling.

Rolling my eyes, I waited until they passed before going in. An arm around my waist had me freezing up, but before I could reach for the knife or the gun attached to the inside of my thighs, a hand came around my mouth with a dirty cloth.

The loud music that was pounding through the building suddenly felt like it was pulsing in my head. I struggled against the stranger's hold, trying to push his hand away, but he was stronger than me and whatever was on that nasty cloth was making me weak. I screamed, but it was muffled.

Suddenly, everything was dark.

Ciro

"No one has seen him, *capo*. He's gone completely ghost on me."

I didn't have time to worry about Volkov disappearing off the face of the planet. It had been three days since I'd told Scarlett about Volkov's wife. Three days since I'd last spoken to her because she'd been avoiding me. Three days in which no one had seen Adrian.

Part of me wondered if Victoria had killed him and dropped his body in the Hudson, but a bigger part didn't give a fuck if he was dead or not. I had too much shit to take care of so I could have five minutes alone with Scarlett and figure out what the hell had happened between the time I'd left her bed and then delivered the information she'd wanted.

"Vito's lost his eyes on him too and I couldn't care less about that motherfucker. Get out there and help the MC assholes find Santino." I didn't wait for him to speak before I hung up and pocketed my phone.

"They're only assholes seventy-five percent of the time, you know."

I ignored my cousin's teasing tone as I paced across my mother's living room to look out at the night sky through the window. It was raining and any other time I liked the kind of storm that was brewing, but tonight I felt like the thunder and lightning that were building up was inside of *me*.

"Relax," Felicity urged from her seat on the couch. "You're giving yourself premature gray hair by worrying."

That she could pick up on my unease meant I hadn't been able to mask it, and I couldn't afford to let many people know I was worried.

"Call her. You'll feel a million times better once you've heard her voice."

She was right. Part of my problem was that I hadn't heard Scarlett's voice in three days. I'd gotten used to seeing her, talking to her daily in the short time she'd been home. My obsessive addiction for her had only doubled since she'd gotten back and having to be without her presence was wearing on my nerves. If I'd had any lingering doubts that I should finally take what was mine, they were gone now.

Instead of reaching for my phone, however, I just glared out at the rain-filled night as my mood turned darker and darker with each beat of my racing heart.

Felicity went back to reading the book she'd been interested in when I'd arrived, ignoring my presence in the room.

My phone vibrated in my pocket and without taking my eyes off the night sky, I pulled it out and lifted it to my ear. "Donati."

"Ciro?" I heard loud music in the background so it took me a moment to recognize the voice. When it did, my blood ran cold. She never called me. Unlike her twin, Victoria didn't seek out my help. She went to Cristiano because she could manipulate him into almost anything. If she was calling me, something was definitely wrong. "Ciro, I can't find Scarlett."

"Victoria, where the fuck are you?"

"Some club downtown," she snapped, sounding stressed. "Scarlett went to the bathroom more than fifteen minutes ago and I can't find her. She dropped her phone."

"Are you stupid?" I roared.

"Don't fucking yell at me. Nothing's ever happened to us before. Just…please, come help me find her, Ciro. I'm starting to get worried." There was a slight quiver in her voice now and I realized she was scared.

"I'm on my way," I told her as I jogged out of my mother's house. "What club?" She named it and I gritted my teeth when I realized it was one that Santino was known to pick up women in. "Don't move, damn it."

"Hurry," she commanded, and I ran faster.

Scarlett wouldn't just wander off from her twin. If Victoria couldn't find her there was a reason, and every one of them had my heart turning to ice in my chest.

My car was parked in front of the house and I got in and left tread marks as I pulled out into traffic. Fifteen minutes, that was how long Victoria said Scarlett had been gone. Fifteen fucking minutes. That was a lifetime. She could be anywhere by now.

With anyone.

As I weaved through traffic, I called Desi. "Get the security footage for the Red Prism. I don't care who you have to bribe, fuck, or kill. I want everything they have."

"They might have it on a Wi-Fi feed that I can hack, *capo*. Give me twenty minutes." Desi hung up and I laid down on the gas.

With each minute it took to get to the club my heart beat harder, faster. I called Paco, told him to get his ass to the Red Prism and take every man we had with him. I didn't want to call Cristiano yet, or Vito, but I called my father and told him to be ready because I knew shit was about to get ugly.

By the time I reached the club I was sure I was on the verge of a heart attack. My hands were clammy, my face covered in sweat, and I couldn't fucking breathe because of the weight that was pressing down on my chest. I found Victoria immediately, since she'd shut the entire club down. The bouncers were guiding people out, while Victoria stood in the middle of the club, her face pale and her eyes wild.

Seeing me enter, she ran across the room and threw herself against me. I didn't have time to comfort her. Grabbing her shoulders, I made her meet my gaze. "Tell me everything."

She swallowed hard. "We danced for about an hour. A few guys tried to dance with us but she wouldn't let them. They lost interest after a while. Then she had to use the bathroom and walked me to the bar so I could get some water before she left me. I haven't seen her since. I checked the bathroom, and found her phone. No one can remember seeing her."

I pushed her away before I did something stupid. Like shake the life out of her for being so careless. How could she let Scarlett just go off unaccompanied like that? They knew better than to go anywhere alone. Fuck, they shouldn't have even left the compound. Vito had told them repeatedly that they needed to stay close to home especially with Santino running around unchecked.

My phone buzzed and I pulled it out. "You'd better have news for me."

"I got the feed," Desi was quick to assure me. "I found Scarlett on there, *capo*. Saw her go into the bathroom and what looks like a guy in black follow her in. Don't see her again until five minutes later from the back entrance feed where he was carrying her to a van. The guys size is close to Santino Jr's. It's probably him."

"Fuck," I roared, causing Victoria and several of the club's security guys to jump.

Someone had taken her, just as I'd feared but had prayed I was overreacting. No, not just someone. Jr. I walked away from Victoria and the other people, trying to breathe through my suddenly tight throat.

Fuck. Fuck. FUCK.

I'd never been scared before. Never really understood terror until right in that moment. I was the boogeyman everyone was scared of, but right then I was about to fall on my knees. Nothing could happen to Scarlett. If I lost her, they might as well kill me too.

Breathe, I mentally commanded myself. *Breathe*. I sucked in a deep breath and clenched my hands into fists. There was no time to break down and act like a pussy. I had to find her.

I would find her.

Chapter 13

Ciro

Two hours. Three minutes. Fifteen… sixteen… seventeen seconds.

Each second that passed, my heart beat four times. She'd been missing for two hours. Two. Fucking. Hours.

I'd already gone through five men to find answers.

None of them had given me what I wanted.

None of them had lived to lie to me again.

Every one of my men was out looking for her, for any sign of Jr. For some miracle that she was still even alive. Vito and my father had joined me while Cristiano was out looking for his sister with his own men. Desi was searching traffic and ATM cameras. He'd been able to hack into Santino Senior's financials, but there was no sign of any New York activity on them.

We were coming up empty-handed and with each ticking of the clock, I became colder. Deadlier.

I'd flipped a switch, turned off everything so that I could focus on getting Scarlett back. If I hadn't, I would have gone insane by now and killed every person who so much as looked at me. I was a cold, emotionless monster and right then I didn't care who had to die to give me what I wanted.

I was scaring my own men, had made one of my father's piss his pants as I'd attempted to beat information out of one man after another. My knuckles were bruised and bleeding. I was pretty sure my left hand was broken, but I didn't feel the pain. The man I'd broken it on wasn't even recognizable now but soon there wouldn't be a body to have to identify. I kept a full supply of acid in the warehouse and soon he would be nothing more than a tub of goo that my men would dump into the Hudson.

"Where the fuck is Volkov?" Vito thundered as he paced through the warehouse where my men had dragged the last idiot who had dared to lie to my face. Vito was pale, his entire frame seeming to tremble as he moved. His children were his kryptonite, but Scarlett was his biggest weakness of all. Scarlett was his favorite child and I couldn't blame him for picking her over the other two.

She was my favorite too.

No one had been able to reach the Russian. If it were for any other reason but finding Scarlett, I wouldn't have even bothered with the bastard, but he had a few different resources than I did. He could help me find her and, by God, he would too or I'd put my knife through his heart.

I'd forced Victoria to call him, knowing he would talk to her. She hadn't hesitated, willing to do anything if it meant getting her twin back. Her fingers had been shaking as she'd dialed, her teeth chattering as she spoke quietly to him.

"I need your help," she'd whispered brokenly as I'd stood beside her like a warden.

That was all it had taken. Volkov had put his resources to good use and said he would call her back. Twenty minutes later Anya had shown up at the club and taken Victoria with her. I hadn't questioned it. Victoria was not my concern. I barely tolerated her and only then because she was Scarlett's sister.

Vito didn't even seem to care that she was with Anya. Whether he was as pissed at her as I was, he just didn't care, or no one else was on his mind right then, I didn't know. I didn't care.

My father put a hand on Vito's shoulder's to steady him. "He will call as soon as he has something."

Vito paused, sucked in a deep breath and nodded. His dark eyes went straight to me. "Are you ready?"

"Yes." I was beyond ready. As soon as Volkov called I would be out the door with six of my men and all the MC guys. Jet was on standby with his brothers and I had plenty of guns to go around. All I needed was a name. A location. Anything to point me in the right direction.

"Good." He nodded again, his face turning into the same blank mask Scarlett had learned to perfect. "You go get her and you bring her home to me. And when you're done, you'd better fucking marry her or I'm going to gut you like a fucking fish."

I didn't even try to pretend I was shocked. I wasn't. Vito might have helped me put distance between me and his daughter, but he'd always known I loved her. It wouldn't have mattered if he'd told me to marry her or not. I was going to. As soon as I had her back I was putting a ring on her finger and making sure no one ever doubted she belonged to me.

Especially her.

Vito's phone went off and he jerked it up to his ear. "Vitucci," he growled, then listened for a long pause. I saw the way his eyes dilated, his nose flared. "Got it. Keep your eyes on the place."

Lowering his hand, he met my gaze. "Go get my daughter, Ciro."

The switch I'd turned off tried to come back on. A small margin of relief filled me, but I quickly banked it down. Volkov had found where she was. That didn't mean she was just sitting around being pampered in the lap of luxury. She could be hurt…or worse.

I pushed that thought aside and turned my emotions off again. She wasn't dead. She couldn't be because my heart was still beating in my chest. I grabbed the two duffel bags full of guns that I always kept packed. Outside, I handed them both over to Paco and jumped in the driver's seat of the SUV.

I didn't wait to see if my men followed. They would. As I drove, Paco sent a text to Jet after I told him the address Vito had given me. The closer I got, the colder I grew until I was nothing more than a flesh-and-blood robot.

I found Volkov on an old abandoned road twenty minutes later. We were just outside the city and the drive would have normally taken close to an hour, but I'd hauled ass. Pulling to a stop beside the older model van where Volkov was sitting behind the driver's seat with four of his men, I looked around for a sign of where Scarlett might be.

"Where the fuck is she?" I demanded as I got out.

There were no buildings that I could see. The road didn't even look like a road any more, but part of the overgrown fields that surrounded it. Thinking that this was just a setup and that Volkov had wasted valuable time that Scarlett might not have, I went for his throat.

"The house is about a mile up the road," Volkov said with calm coolness. "Jr isn't with them, but there are seven or so men outside the house. I'm not sure how many are inside. If it were just the seven, my men and I could have handled it ourselves, but I didn't want to put her at risk in case I was wrong."

I sucked in a harsh breath just as the sound of another vehicle filled my ears. I glanced away long enough to confirm that it was the MC guys, then turned back to Volkov. "How big is the house?"

"It's a small farmhouse. One story. Old and decaying. The place belongs to one of Santino's mistresses." I didn't even try to second guess that information. I knew Jr had a few mistresses, but the few I knew of and had questioned hadn't known shit. Obviously Volkov had better intel than I did. "There are two entrances. The front door, of course, and the back door that is right off the kitchen. There are men posted at both doors, with the others walking the perimeter."

Jet and his brothers had joined us by the time he was finished. No one spoke, just listened.

"Paco, you and two of the Hannigans take the front door. Jet, you and Hawk come with me." They were better shots so I wanted them with me. "The rest of you take out the other men. But be careful where you put a bullet. We don't know where Scarlett is in the house and I don't want her hit by a stray."

"We will help you," Volkov informed me as I pulled out three guns and a flashlight. I tucked them into my belt and then grabbed a sawed-off shotgun. This was my favorite because it could put a hole the size of a bowling ball in a man's chest.

I wanted to tell him to fuck off. His job was done. I'd found Scarlett. But as he'd said before, there was no way of knowing how many men were in the house. I wouldn't put her at risk by turning him down. "You and one of your men come with me. The others can go with Paco."

I grabbed a box of bullets and started loading. Once everyone was armed, we quietly made our way through the field, keeping to the dark shadows since the moon had come out after it had stopped raining. There were enough trees to keep us out of the line of sight.

Paco and the other men moved into place first, and we moved toward the house. Santino's men must have been half asleep, because when I put my gun to the first fucker's head, he jerked in surprise. I saw a flash of fear and pulled the trigger, watching as his brains hit the side of the house behind him.

From the front of the house I heard guns going off. Men cursed, some in Italian, others in English, but they didn't last long. Beside me, Jet put a bullet in a man that came running from the front of the house. The man dropped to his knees and then fell on his face, the life draining out of him as he bled onto the rain-slickened ground.

Hawk opened the door and entered first, calling an all-clear before the rest of us entered. There were no other men inside, though. Each room we came to was empty. No furniture. Not even any electricity. The house smelled like dank rotten wood, week-old garbage, and stale cigarette smoke. I could hear mice and rats in the walls and walked into a dozen spider webs before we'd even cleared the kitchen.

Each room we checked, we came up empty. As each minute ticked by, I grew more and more tense. My finger itched to pull the trigger on my gun, to put a hole through something—or preferably through Jr.

There was only one more room to check. Not wanting to scare her, I stopped Jet and Hawk at the door. "Stay here. I don't want to startle her."

"She might not even be in there," Hawk told me in a low, rough voice. "Volkov might have gotten it wrong."

"I didn't," Adrian growled. "She's here. I swear to you she's here, Donati. I wouldn't risk Victoria's sister like that."

I held up my flashlight, shining it in their eyes, shutting them all up. "She's here." I could feel her.

Reaching behind me, I turned the doorknob and stepped back. Keeping my flashlight pointed down, I slowly stepped inside the room. The smells weren't as bad in here, but the smoke lingered more there than any other room. Trying not to scare her, I lifted the flashlight until I saw the bed.

Her feet were tied to the corners at the end of the bed. As I shifted the light, I saw that her dress was still on. I'd seen the aftereffect of a girl Jr had raped before. She had been a bloody mess, with her clothes slashed off. He'd destroyed her emotionally as well as physically and the girl had committed suicide while still in the hospital recovering. As far as I could see in the dim lighting, Scarlett hadn't been sexually assaulted.

That wouldn't save Jr from me, but I was thankful all the same.

"Ciro!" she cried, and I moved closer to the bed, still trying not to scare her. I wanted to fall on my knees then and there and thank God that she was alive, but first I had to get her out of that disgusting place.

"Is Victoria here?" she demanded, sounding a little unnerved.

"She's safe," I assured her.

"Thank God," she whispered.

I was trying to keep the switch to my emotions off, but with each inch of her I revealed that was becoming harder and harder to do. My hands shook, causing the flashlight to flicker across her chest. Her arms were over her head, but it was her face that I couldn't look away from. Her eyes were bright with pain, and no wonder. Her beautiful face was one big bruise. As I drew closer I could actually see his hand prints on her face.

"Please put the light down," she moaned. "I think I have a concussion and it's making me sick."

"Baby…" I dropped the flashlight on the bed and reached for the cable ties that were keeping her hands tied to the headboard. Pulling out my knife, I made quick work of freeing her. A whimper seemed to be torn from her as I slowly lowered her arms to the bed.

"I might have broken ribs," she told me in a pained voice and I noticed how shallow her breathing was.

"Fuck," I growled. My eyes went back to her face, tracing over each bruise. Her eyes were slightly swollen, but she seemed to be able to see. Her lip was busted, but it had stopped bleeding for the moment. She would need a few stitches.

The motherfucker had beaten her and it was taking everything inside of me not to hunt him down then and there and tear him apart with my bare hands. I had to take care of Scarlett first. She came first.

Once her legs were untied, I lifted her into my arms. The pained sounds that left her gutted me. "I'm sorry, baby." I pressed a kiss to her temple.

"I have to pee," she whispered.

"Okay." I picked up the flashlight and carried her to the door. "Where's the bathroom?" I asked the men still standing there, their guns at the ready.

"It was down the hall," Jet said as he led the way. "Here." Opening the door he shined his flashlight inside. "It's pretty nasty in there though, man."

"I'm going to make a mess if I don't pee soon," Scarlett moaned.

"It's okay. I'll help you," I promised and stepped around the biker. With her still tucked in my arms, I put the flashlight down on the old sink that looked like it was covered in mold and smelled just as dank as the rest of the house.

"Put me down," she urged. "I'll be okay."

"Not if you have a concussion. I'll help you, baby." I shifted her in my arms, my fingers sliding under her dress and finding her panties.

I tried not to think about what I was doing, where I was touching her. Her outer thigh was silky soft, her ass warm and tight as my fingers skimmed over one cheek. It was harder than I ever could have imagined, but I kept a firm hold on myself as I pulled her underwear down and her dress up.

"Well, this isn't embarrassing at all," she muttered.

I pressed another kiss to her temple, more than a little overwhelmed now that the realization she was alive and actually in my arms was starting to set in. It wasn't easy, but I held her above the toilet seat and she was able to relieve herself without causing a mess. When she was done I straightened her clothes and carried her back out.

Jet, Hawk, and Volkov were still standing where I'd left them on the other side of the door. The rest of my men were outside, and we quickly made our way out to them. The clouds had covered up the moon and it was starting to rain again. Paco, the other two MC guys and Volkov's men were already dealing with the dead bodies.

"Anyone alive?" Volkov asked as he inspected the fallen men.

"One's got a gut wound. He won't make it another hour," Colt Hannigan assured him.

"Good. Let's see if we can get some information out of him." The Russian walked over to the fallen man who was slowly bleeding out.

It would have probably relieved some of my own tension if I helped get information out of the little fucker, but I had more important things to take care of. Scarlett needed a doctor. She was starting to relax against me as the events and her pain caught up to her and she was practically lethargic in my arms. "Paco, stay with Volkov. Keep me informed."

"Don't worry about this shit," Hawk Hannigan muttered beside me. "You take care of your female. We got your back."

I didn't completely believe him. Hawk had just as many reasons to want to find Jr as I did. Jr's men had taken Hawk's girlfriend, which was why he was even in New York. Thankfully we'd found the girl in one piece, but she'd been sick with blood poisoning. She was still in the hospital and Felicity had told me she was making a slow recovery.

"I'm sleepy," Scarlett murmured, cuddling closer before shivering. "And cold."

"Don't go to sleep," I commanded as I started back toward the SUV with two of my other men right behind me. "Keep your eyes open, baby. Talk to me."

"So bossy," she said with a small grunt. "Don't yell at me."

"I'm not yelling. It just feels that way with your head all fuzzy." I quickened my steps but had to be careful with the ground so damp and the rain starting to fall heavily. She was getting soaked. "Stay awake, Scarlett."

"I'm trying."

"Try harder."

She lifted her head to glare at me. Even in the dim lighting from the flashlights, I could see that spark of life flashing back at me. It warmed my heart to see it. "I don't know why I love you, Ciro Donati. You're such a dickhead most of the time."

I felt a smile actually teasing at my lips, and pressed a quick, gentle kiss to the tip of her nose. "I'm just thankful you do love me, Scarlett. That's all I've ever wanted."

"Don't say things like that. I can't tell if you're playing with me or speaking the truth." Her bottom lip pouted out and I had to force myself not to suck that lusciousness into my mouth.

"It's the truth, baby. Every word."

Chapter 14

Scarlett

I hated hospitals. Doctors were kind of creepy if you asked me. They always had cold hands and they talked down to you like you didn't have a brain in your head. Like it was your fault when you got sick or had an accident that required emergency attention.

Because of Victoria's diabetes, she'd had to deal with doctors all her life. She handled having to be pinched and poked on a regular basis like she did most everything else: with a sweet smile on her happy face for the doctor. I hadn't been sick very often and the few times I had been, I tried to hide it so my father wouldn't make me see a doctor. Irresponsible, maybe, but my dislike of anyone with a medical degree hadn't cared.

I didn't have a choice this time. Ciro wasn't likely to take no for an answer, and I hurt so badly that for once I didn't care if I had icy hands poking and prodding as long as they gave me something strong enough to knock me out so I could escape from the headache pulsing behind my eyes. The cracked ribs made it difficult to breathe, but that pain was nothing compared to the headache.

Ciro made having to deal with the arrogant-ass doctor a little easier. The smile the doctor had worn when he'd first entered my private ER room had disappeared the instant he'd set eyes on the beast of a man who refused to leave my side. Because of me, the ER was pretty much shut down.

Ciro's men had sealed off a few private rooms and had refused to let anyone but the doctor near me. Not even the nurses were allowed access. No one had dared to argue. My father had already called and from the tone of his voice, I was pretty sure he was approaching the end of his limit. He hadn't talked to me, but even from where I'd been sitting I could hear the rage in his voice—and the fear. He was on his way and I could honestly say I'd never wanted my Papa more than I did right then.

Within minutes of getting to the ER, I was having x-rays to see how bad my ribs were and the doctor had already diagnosed a concussion. I'd already known that, damn it. A few Vicodin for my headache was all I was really looking for.

"I'm going to admit her for observations," the doctor told Ciro once he had my x-rays back.

"I don't want to stay. I just want to go home," I snapped at the man who had spoken only to Ciro during the thirty minutes I'd been in my room.

It was like I wasn't even there. Honestly, I understood why he'd only been talking to Ciro. He'd taken charge of everything like he normally did, but there was something about him that screamed ‘I will fuck you up’ tonight. Even more so than normal. The doctor had practically pissed himself when he’d first started examining me and I’d been unable to bite back the pained whimpers as he’d checked my ribs. Ciro hadn’t even moved, but the growl that had left him had sounded so animalistic that the guy had actually started to shake.

“If the man thinks you should stay, you’ll stay.” Ciro’s tone didn’t leave room for arguing and my head was hurting too bad for me to try.

“Will you stay with me?” The thought of being alone in a place I didn’t want to be was too much to handle right then. Not just anyone of my father’s men would do, either. It had to be Ciro. He would protect me. He would make sure the doctor didn’t talk down to me. He would keep whoever the hell had done this to me from doing it again.

I put it down to the concussion, not wanting to admit what it really was.

That maybe I was scared.

Ciro turned away from the doctor, his blue eyes softening as he lifted a hand and cupped my aching face. “Baby, I’m not going anywhere. Ever.”

I couldn’t get my voice to work so I just nodded. Stupid concussion. Now I was close to tears for no reason at all.

Carefully, he lowered his hand but claimed mine. His big paw practically swallowed mine, but if anything, that made me feel better.

“We should have a room for her soon, Mr. Donati,” the doctor told him after a moment. “I’ll make arrangements to have your…associates made comfortable."

Ciro's head snapped around, his eyes drilling into the doctor and making the man pale. "You worry about making Scarlett comfortable. My men will be fine." His hold tightened on my hand, but not painfully. "She's in pain. Do something about that instead of kissing my ass."

"Y-yes, sir," he stuttered, then left tread marks on his way out he was moving so fast.

"Well, this has been fun," I muttered with a dry laugh. He glared down at me, his jaw tensing, and I had to laugh again. "You're kind of cute when your nose flares like that."

"Your head must be more fucked up than I thought," he said, shaking his head, but I thought I saw a ghost of a smile teasing at his lips.

"It's killing me right now," I told him, rubbing at my temples with my free hand since he didn't seem to be willing to let me go. I wasn't going to complain.

The door to the exam room opened and the doctor returned just as quickly as he'd left, this time with two syringes in his hand. "This should do the trick," he muttered as he moved around Ciro to get to me, then paused. "I'll have to put it in her hip."

"Of course you will," Ciro gritted out.

Reluctantly, he released my hand and then helped me turn onto my side. I felt his fingers skim up my thigh, pushing my dress up to expose my left hip. Shifting my panties out of the way, he waited until the doctor gave me the shot. I was so distracted by the feel of Ciro's warmth trying to invade my every sense that I didn't feel the sharp prick of the needle. The burn as the medicine went in, however, was too strong to ignore.

"This might upset your stomach, Miss Vitucci. I'm going to give you something for nausea to keep that at a minimum." As he said it, he stuck me with the second needle. This time the burn was less harsh, but it still had my hip aching. He finally put a bandage on and then stepped back. "The combination of the two will probably make her fall asleep. Someone will be in to wake her every two hours because of the concussion."

I was already starting to feel the effects. The pain in my head didn't completely go away, but it was enough that I breathed a sigh of relief. My eyes grew heavy and it was an effort to keep them open. As they started to drift closed, I snapped them back open. The darkness felt like it was trying to swallow me whole.

Ciro retook my hand, his heat seeming to invade my body and ease my racing mind. This time when my eyes refused to cooperate and stay open, I gave up the fight. I was safe with Ciro. He wouldn't let anything happen to me. If nothing else, I at least knew that much.

"Rest, *vita mia*. I've got you."

Ciro

Scarlett's soft breathing was the only sound in the room. Whether she knew it or not, she was practically clinging to my hand in her sleep. She didn't have to. There was no way in hell I was going to let her go.

Behind me the exam room door opened, and I slowly turned to face my father and Vito as they entered the room. Cristiano was right behind them, his mouth already open but I held up my free hand to quieten them all.

"She's sleeping. Don't wake her." I kept my voice low so she wouldn't be disturbed.

Cristiano's mouth snapped shut, his hands thrusting into his pants pockets as he stepped forward to look down at his sister. He was pale, his eyes bloodshot and wild. Between him and Vito, I wasn't sure who was more worried. They both looked like they'd aged a decade.

The three other men seemed to take up most of the space in the little room, but I wasn't about to move away from Scarlett. I wasn't going to let her go for any reason. After only a few minutes, Vito pulled his son away so he could take his place, his eyes tracing over his daughter's face. With each bruise he saw I could feel his tension growing until the room seemed charged with it.

He lifted his head, a cold, blank expression on his face. "I want that bastard dealt with. No excuses."

"We'll get him, Vito," my father assured him, putting his hand on his friend's shoulder. "Let's focus on the fact we got Scarlett back. Santino and his son will get theirs soon enough."

"Not soon enough for me," Vito snapped, then quickly lowered his voice when Scarlett shifted into a more comfortable position. "Do whatever you have to, but make sure that Jr takes his last breath."

"I have every one of my men on it, Vito. Volkov has one of the men from tonight. He'll get some answers." I rubbed my thumb over the back of Scarlett's knuckles, letting her warmth ease some of my own growing tension.

"How the fuck did he know where to find her?" Cristiano muttered as he leaned against the wall by the door.

"I don't know and I don't care. All that matters is that we have your sister back." Vito bent, pressed a tender kiss to her forehead, then quickly moved back. The suit he was wearing was rumbled, his shirt half unbuttoned and his tie gone. This was the most unkempt I'd ever seen Vito in my entire life. Normally he was put together no matter how stressed he was.

Having nearly lost Scarlett was showing on him and I couldn't blame him. I hadn't seen myself in a mirror, but I knew I probably looked just as fucked up as he did.

There was a sharp tap on the door before one of my men stuck his head inside. "There are two nurses out here that say they want to take Miss Vitucci upstairs, boss."

"So they are admitting her?" Vito's face grew gray, unable to hide his worry now.

"Just for observations. Her ribs aren't broken, just badly bruised, but her concussion is something they want to keep an eye on. It's only for twenty-four hours, Vito." I had to keep reminding myself of that. Concussions were tricky. The safest place for her was in the hospital where she could get immediate help if she needed it.

"Let them in," Cristiano told the man.

When the door opened again, two nurses in green scrubs entered. They were both middle-aged, the stress of their jobs showing on their faces as well as the silver that streaked their hair that was pulled into tight buns.

"We're here for Miss Vitucci," the one holding a chart said as she offered us a sympathetic smile.

"We're coming with her," Vito informed her.

"I don't think—" the other nurse started, but Vito quickly cut her off.

"I'm not really concerned with what you think," he snapped, causing them both to pale and Scarlett to shift restlessly. "We will be accompanying my daughter. Someone will be with her at all times and my men will be stationed outside her room."

"Yes sir," the first nurse murmured. "We will be happy to accommodate your daughter's needs. May we take her up now?"

He stared them down long and hard, but then stepped aside to let them closer. When they saw how badly Scarlett's face was bruised, they were unable to contain their surprised gasps. The second nurse opened her mouth, but a cold look from Vito had her biting her tongue.

"Sir…" The first nurse was beside me now. "You're going to have to release her."

"Fuck that. I'll help you, but I'm not letting her go."

"Son, the nurses are only doing their jobs." My father tried to be the reasonable one, but I didn't even look at him.

I. Wasn't. Letting. Her. Go.

She shifted again, her hand tightening around my own and I looked down to find her eyes wide open. "What's wrong?"

I stroked a finger down her cheek. "Nothing. Go back to sleep."

She didn't listen. She never did. Her brown eyes went around the room. "Papa," she whispered a little shakily, and Vito was beside her in the blink of an eye.

"How are you feeling, *passerotta*?"

A smile lifted at the corners of her mouth. "I'm pretty high right now, Papa." She blinked, the smile slowly fading before it had even really formed as she finally saw how bad Vito looked. "Don't worry about me, Papa. I'm fine now. Ciro has been taking great care of me."

He tapped her on the nose like he always did. "I know that, *passerotta*. There's no one I would trust you with but him."

"We should get her upstairs now." The nurse who was still holding the chart spoke quietly. "She will be more comfortable up there."

Scarlett's fingers tightened again, her eyes widening as she took note of the nurses. "Not without Ciro."

I lifted her hand to my lips. "I swear to you I'm not going anywhere."

I watched helplessly as her chin started to tremble, but she quickly reined in her emotions and gave a small nod. "O-okay."

The nurses weren't happy, but we managed to get her upstairs without me releasing Scarlett's hand. The private room was only slightly bigger than the ER exam room, and with the nurses taking vitals and attempting to make her comfortable, plus four large men, there was no room to move around.

I knew she didn't like all the people in there with her when she was feeling so vulnerable. "I'm sure Ma wants to know how Scarlett is," I told my father. "Maybe you should call her."

My father took the hint. Smiling adoringly down at Scarlett, he moved close to give her a quick kiss on the forehead. "I'm glad you're okay, sweetheart."

"Thanks, *Zio* Ben," she murmured.

"Cristiano, go check on Victoria," Vito commanded, realizing why I was getting rid of my father and sending his son away to make it easier on Scarlett.

"She's at Anya's place, Papa. She's perfectly safe and fine where she is."

Vito glared at his son. "I want you to go and check for yourself. If your eyes aren't on her, then how do you know she's fine?"

Blowing out a frustrated breath, Cristiano nodded. "You're right." Reluctantly he moved so he could bend over and kiss his sister the same way my father had. "I love you, Scarlett."

"I love you too," she said into his chest as he hugged her. "Give Tor a kiss for me."

Once the two were gone, the room felt bigger and Scarlett relaxed a little more. After a few more minutes the nurses left us alone and she finally started to let her eyes drift shut once again.

Vito pulled two chairs over to the bed. I took one, still holding tight to her small hand. We sat together watching Scarlett sleep for a long while before Vito spoke again.

"I said I wanted you to handle Jr, but the more I sit here thinking of how strong Scarlett is, I know that I can't allow you to be the one to end him."

My blood ran cold as a sinking suspicion filled me. "It's my right to take care of that little motherfucker."

Vito lifted his eyes from his daughter's sleeping face. He looked at me for a long time, his face blank, but then shook his head. "It's Scarlett's right, Ciro. She deserves the chance to put a bullet between his eyes. No one but her."

"No."

I wouldn't let her bloody her hands, not even to end the man who had hurt her. That was why she had me. It was my right—my fucking privilege—to take care of her in every way possible. That included slaughtering the man who had dared to beat her.

"All her life, you've been so unyielding about keeping her and Victoria as far away from this side of your life," I tried to reason with him, feeling like Scarlett's soul was on the line. "Don't pull her into it now, Vito. Don't make her like me."

Understanding filled his eyes and he shook his head. "My boy, I know you love my daughter, but you've really let yourself turn a blind eye to her true nature. I know she's come to you for things in the past. You've helped her more times than I really want to know, but if she hadn't had you how do you think she would have accomplished those things?"

I didn't want to think about not being there for her when she'd needed me in the past.

Vito sighed at my stony silence. "She is just as capable of doing those things herself, Ciro. I love that girl more than anyone else in the world. Maybe it's because she's so strong that I've let myself play favorites between her and Victoria. I don't know. What I do know is that if she'd been born before Cristiano, I would have happily turned everything over to her when I die."

"I don't deny her strength, damn it. It was what drew me to her in the first place." I lifted her hand and brushed a kiss over her knuckles. "It's the blood, Vito. The blood I've spilled stains my soul. Don't let that happen to Scarlett."

"I'll let her decide," he said, sounding as if he was going to give her a choice. We both knew what her decision would be if she was given one. "I owe her that much at least."

Chapter 15

Scarlett

Each time a nurse came in, I was in a deep sleep thanks to the drugs the doctor had given me. Each time I had to open my eyes, Ciro was still sitting in a chair beside my bed, my hand safely tucked in his own. Whether he knew it or not, he kept stroking his thumb over the back of my hand, but when the nurse left I was able to find peace in sleep again because of it.

Papa was still there when I finally gave up on sleep the next morning after the last time a new nurse had come in. There was a tension in the room and from the look on Ciro's pale, scruffy face I could tell he wasn't happy about something. Figuring it was because he had to babysit me, I sat up and pulled my hand free.

"When can I go home?" I asked my father, who was watching me with concerned eyes. If my face looked half as bad as it felt, I could completely understand his worry. My face hurt more today than it had the night before. Between that pain and the headache that were fighting for my attention, I was one massive ache.

"When the doctor determines that you're well enough," Ciro said with a growl.

"I want to go home now." I snuck a glance at Ciro, saw his face was set in stone, and quickly looked away.

Some of the things I'd said to him the night before were starting to come back to me, and I wanted to disappear. Had I really told him I loved him? Had he really said he was thankful that I did, or had my concussion made me imagine that? Shit, had I really peed while he held me above some nasty-smelling toilet?

I didn't know and I needed some time and space away from everything else so I could try to remember. Or forget. "Please, Papa. I hate it here. How am I supposed to get well if I'm not comfortable with my surroundings?"

He seemed to think that over for a moment, then stood. "Okay, *passerotta*." He bent and kissed the top of my head. "I'll see what I can do."

"Thank you, Papa."

He shook his head. "Anything for you."

As the door shut behind him, Ciro unfolded his large body from the chair he'd been in all night. I decided that the wrinkles in my blanket were more interesting to look at than him and refused to lift my gaze as he moved to stand beside me. His hand touched the mattress beside my head as he bent. I swallowed the lump that filled my throat when I felt his lips touch the top of my head, but didn't dare look at him again.

"Scarlett, look at me," he commanded in a low voice.

"How is Victoria?" I ignored his harsh exhale. I couldn't do this with him right now. I just couldn't. Everything was too raw for me. My emotions were close to the surface and the things I felt for this man were too jumbled in my concussed head to really make sense of them right then.

"As far as I know, she's fine," Ciro assured me after a moment where I imagined him glaring at the top of my head. "Cristiano went to check on her and I haven't heard from him since."

"Did you say she was at Anya's?" I pushed the hair back from my face, unsettled that my sister was with Adrian's sister. Too many things were wrong with that, too many things could go wrong. She should have been home, not somewhere Adrian could get his hands on her and fill her head with lies once again.

"Yes."

"I need to talk to her. She's probably losing her mind right now." If it had been her in my place, I knew I would have gone insane with the need to see with my own eyes that she was safe.

"She's fine," he said again.

"I want to talk to her," I repeated, finally looking up at him and meeting his guarded eyes with a glare that would send any other person running for shelter from my temper. "Can I use your phone?"

"No. You can speak to your sister later. After you've gotten home where you seem so determined to go." He bent until his face was only a few inches from my own. "Now stop thinking those stupid things that have been going through your head since you woke up a little while ago."

His eyes trapped my own and I couldn't have looked away if my life had depended on it. "I don't know what you mean."

We both knew I was lying.

Ciro moved half an inch closer and I could taste his breath on my lips. My mouth fell open, seeming to have a mind of its own and craving more of his taste. "As soon as you're better, we are going to sit down and have a long overdue talk, baby. Until then, stop overthinking the things you and I both said last night."

"I have a concussion. Whatever I did or didn't say last night wasn't true."

He moved so close his nose brushed against my own. "I pray that you're lying, Scarlett. Because what you said to me has been the only thing that has kept me from losing my mind all night." He pressed his lips to the corner of my mouth. I closed my eyes, loving the feel of his lips against me. "As hard as I've fought how I feel for you, part of me has always known that you are the only thing in this world that I could call mine."

"No," I tried to deny, but my heart was going crazy with the possibility that what he was saying was the truth.

"You're mine and I'm yours," he murmured, his tongue teasing at my bottom lip. "I'm tired of fighting it and I refuse to do it ever again."

I leaned into his kiss when he sucked my bottom lip into his mouth. My hands went to his chest, my fingers fisting in his shirt, desperate to keep him close, scared he was playing with me and would pull away at any minute. That's what he'd done in the past. Given me just a taste of what I could have with him, only to push me away and run as fast as he could in the opposite direction. I didn't know if I could trust this now, but I wanted it more than I wanted my next breath.

If he was playing with me this time, I wasn't sure I'd ever get over it. Not with everything so upside down inside my head.

"I won't let you go this time, *vita mia*," he said as he released my lips and pressed his forehead against mine. His breathing came in harsh pants. "Don't push me away."

My fingers tightened in his shirt. "Does this seem like I'm pushing?"

"No, but as soon as I give you room to breathe, you'll be thinking stupid shit again."

"So don't let me breathe." I tugged him closer. "Kiss me again."

The kiss was short but made me more lightheaded than the drugs the doctor had put in me the night before. When he pulled back, his eyes were dark with a need that matched my own. I couldn't wrap my head around what had just happened, but for now I was going to go with it. For too long I'd wanted this with Ciro and when I'd thought it was out of my reach, he was pulling me in with a taste of a fantasy I'd been holding on to since I was eleven years old.

"Scarlett..." He carefully kissed my forehead, then moved back just enough so he could meet my eyes. "Promise me something."

"You know I can't do that unless I know what I'm promising to do."

He grimaced. "Promise me you'll let me deal with Santino. No matter what your father says, I need to take care of this. Please?"

Maybe my head was more affected than I'd realized, because that made no sense to me. I opened my mouth to ask what he was talking about, but my father opened the door and came in with a man in a lab coat right behind him. "This nice doctor has decided to let you go home a few hours early, *passerotta*," Papa said with a hard look in the doctor's direction. "Right?"

Ciro straightened, turning his full attention on the newcomer, but he kept his hand beside my head. Always protecting me.

The doctor, a man in his late thirties, had the beginnings of a receding hair line and was more on the short side of six feet. From his accent I knew he hadn't been born in the US, but it wasn't so thick I couldn't understand him. "Miss Vitucci, it's against my better judgment to discharge you before the full twenty-four hours are up, but your father has assured me that you will have the best care money can buy waiting for you at home. Is that true?"

"If my father said that, then it's true." I barely spared the man another glance. "Papa, I need clean clothes." All I had on was a thin hospital gown. I had no idea where my dress was, or even where my underwear was, and I didn't really care. But there was no way I was leaving that room in a damn gown.

"Mary is on her way," he assured me. "She can help you dress when she gets here."

"I'll release you into your father's care, Miss Vitucci." The doctor forced my attention back to him. "But you will have to take it easy for the next few days at the very least. Staying in bed would be ideal."

"I'll make sure she stays there." Ciro was quickly turning back into his domineering self, not that I was going to complain. I liked his assertiveness.

Most of the time.

Chapter 16

Ciro

Scarlett was set to get home. Even though I had wanted her to stay for at least a few more hours at the hospital, we were now back at the compound. We'd taken Vito's car and I'd sat in the back with her the entire ride home.

As soon as the car came to a stop she was reaching for her door. "Will you please just let me help you?" I grumbled as I climbed out and then reached back inside for her.

"I can walk. Despite how hideous I look this morning, my legs still work," she complained as I carried her into the house, but her arms were wrapped around my neck so tight I knew her bitching was more for show than actually wanting me to put her down.

"You couldn't be hideous if you tried, *vita mia*," I assured her as I pressed my lips to her forehead.

Pleasure filled her brown eyes. "When did you get so charming?"

I found myself grinning. "Right around the time you turned seventeen." I winked and she sucked in a sharp breath.

That quickly I found my body hardening for her. One little gasp that told me she wanted me and I was ready to bend her over and slide into her heat. That wasn't going to happen anytime soon, though. She was sore and hurting despite the meds the doctor had given her before we'd left the hospital.

The guards all stopped to watch me as I tucked her closer. I had never let them see this part of me. Fuck, I had never let them see anything but the cold robotic-like machine I was supposed to be when I was working. I shot them a cold glare and they seemed to scatter. Scarlett lifted a brow at me, smirked, but didn't say a word as I took the stairs two at a time.

Vito was somewhere behind us, but when one of his men stopped him, I kept going without him. The less time he was with Scarlett the better. I didn't want to give him the chance to even *make* the offer we'd argued over the night before.

In her room, I placed her in the middle of her bed and then tucked the covers up around her. Straightening, I tossed the contents of my pockets on her nightstand and dropped down beside her. Fuck, her bed was comfortable. I hadn't slept any the night before and now that Scarlett was home I could actually relax a little. Exhaustion was already trying to swallow me.

She shifted closer to me, her head going automatically to my chest, her left hand resting over my heart. “This is nice,” she said with a tired sigh. “I like it.”

Pressing my lips to the top of her head, I smiled. “Yeah, *vita mia*. I like it too.”

In only a matter of minutes I felt her breathing evening out and knew she was asleep. The meds the doctor had given her before we’d left the hospital hadn’t been as hardcore as the ones from the night before, but they were strong enough to take the major part of the edge off and help her rest.

With her warmth flooding into me and her slight weight pressed against me, I quickly found sleep myself…

All too soon my phone was ringing. Fuck. I didn’t want to move. I’d only experienced sleep that peaceful the night I’d slept in this same bed with Scarlett tucked against me.

Scarlett shifted beside me. “Make it stop,” she groaned.

Pressing a kiss to her head, I reached for the phone. “Go back to sleep, baby.” Grabbing the nosy thing, I lifted it to my ear without bothering to open my eyes to see who it was. “Donati,” I snapped to whomever had been stupid enough to wake me up.

“We got some new artwork downtown, *capo*,” Paco told me.

Fuck. I didn’t want to leave Scarlett. I was more comfortable than I’d been in weeks and the feel of her still against me was almost too much to resist. But when there was ‘artwork’ downtown, I knew I had shit to take care of. "I'll be there in thirty."

Dropping the phone back on the nightstand, I shifted so Scarlett was still lying on my arm, but I was leaning over her. She looked up at me through her lashes and my entire body instantly became one massive throb. Hell, I wanted to slide between her legs then and there and from that look on her beautiful, sleepy face, I knew she wanted it just as badly as I did.

I didn't have to be present for what was going on at the warehouse. Paco could handle it. Why the fuck would I want to leave this bed—leave my woman—to deal with whatever was waiting on me downtown?

"You need to go," she murmured, sensing my reluctance to leave her.

"I don't want to," I told her honestly.

A grin teased at her lips. "I don't want you to, either. But I know that was important. Go. I'll still be here when you get back."

She wasn't asking questions. Wasn't complaining that I had to leave. She was urging me to go and promising to be right there when I was done. Not many women would do that. Not many would accept that there were things I couldn't tell her. They couldn't accept the fact that I would probably come home with another man's blood on my hands.

Fuck. Why had I wasted so much time running away from this woman when it was obvious she was made for me? I was a goddamn idiot, that was why. I'd wasted so much time by pushing her away when we could have been happy together all along.

Lowering my head, I kissed her lips, being careful not to cause her bruised face any more pain. She tasted of honey with just the trace of mint. My dick flexed against the zipper of my jeans, the metal biting into my flesh and letting me know loud and clear that I either needed to take care of business, or stay and take what I was so desperate for.

Scarlett was the one to pull away first. Her long fingers cupped my jaw, her breaths coming in little pants. "Go, Ciro. But come back to me as soon as you're done."

***

Artwork meant Paco had someone at the warehouse downtown for me to question. Most of the time, questioning turned into an all-out bloodbath and by the time I was done it looked like I'd been playing in red paint. Tonight, I wasn't the one doing the questioning.

I stared down at the man lying on the metal table with his arms stretched above his head and his legs strapped down tightly. He stared sightlessly at the ceiling and if it weren't for the fact his chest was lifting and falling with each gasp he took, I would have thought he was dead.

At the head of the table, Hawk Hannigan held a blade to the man's throat, teasing him with the thought of slitting it. He'd been itching to stick his knife in someone since he'd stepped off a plane weeks ago. Now he was getting the chance and relishing every second of it.

Hawk had already sliced and diced the guy's chest, cut off one of his pinkies, and his left ear. The scent of blood filled the back room of the warehouse where I took care of business of this nature. The screams hadn't turned into pleas yet, and I wondered what the fuck this guy was on if he could withstand that much pain without passing out. Jr was an addict so it wouldn't surprise me if his men were too. Whatever it was, it wasn't enough to stop him from crying. Tears fell down his cheeks in rivers, but still he remained quiet.

Volkov had gotten a lead on Jr when he'd questioned the guy with the gut wound the night before. That poor sonofabitch hadn't lasted long enough to do more than breathe the only address he could think of. Volkov, Paco, and the MC guys hadn't found Jr there, but his second-in-command—Fontana—was just as good. We would make the bastard talk, give up where his boss was hiding out like the coward he was.

As soon as Jr had taken his last breath, I'd be able to relax a little more. Until then I had to worry about Scarlett's safety and whether Vito would actually give her the opportunity to end Jr herself. I could only pray I was able to get it taken care of before Vito was able to make that particular offer to his daughter. I'd worry about Vito being pissed later, but I couldn't let Scarlett take so much as a step down that road. She might understand me having to handle things like this, but she didn't know what it felt like to end someone's life.

I was able to turn that part of myself off when I needed to. Scarlett wouldn't be able to do the same thing. She was tough and stronger than any other woman I knew, even my mother. That was one of the things I loved about her, but I knew she wouldn't be the same if she took another person's life.

Hawk skimmed the blade of his wicked-looking knife down the man's cheek. "Where is Santino?" he asked in a voice that was oddly quiet, almost like he was trying to soothe the guy he had just carved up like a turkey.

No answer. He didn't even open his mouth.

Jet Hannigan stepped up beside the guy's hands. Using a pair of pliers, he pulled out two of the guy's fingernails. The room filled with Fontana's screams once again, but no one outside would have heard him. The place was deserted, but even if it hadn't been, the building was soundproof. When they stopped, Hawk spoke again. "What was that? I couldn't hear you over some pussy squealing like a pig."

"Just kill me." Fontana groaned weakly, his will to live gone now as he slowly bled out on the floor. "Kill me."

"Nah, that's too easy. We'll pump you full of fresh blood if we have to, but you won't be meeting the Angel of Death anytime soon." Hawk scratched his scruffy chin and glanced around the room. "I'm bored with this. Who's next?"

Several other men shifted restlessly, wanting to go a few rounds with Fontana, but waiting to see if I would step in. I didn't even move. Fontana wasn't who I wanted, but if I took a turn the fucker would be dead in half an hour.

Volkov and Cristiano had both been standing quietly beside me as we watched, but it was the former who took Hawk's place. I'd heard plenty of rumors about the Russian's methods of getting people to talk, but up until right then I'd never believed them. I should have. My sources hadn't exaggerated. Hell, if anything they had left a lot of the details out.

I always turned a part of myself off when I did this kind of work, but Volkov seemed to turn a part of himself on. He even smiled, as if he actually enjoyed it. I'd always had a little respect for the man, but right then he made me feel uneasy.

Cristiano shifted with his own apprehension beside me. We hadn't talked about either of his sisters other than to say they were each safe. He'd been at Anya's with Victoria since the night before as far as I knew. Whatever was going on with the younger twin, she wasn't in a rush to get back to the compound and, surprisingly, no one seemed to be forcing her to head home either. I hadn't shared with my friend what Scarlett had asked me to find out, but that didn't mean Cristiano didn't know his favorite sister had been seeing Volkov until I'd given Scarlett the information she had wanted.

Jet Hannigan raised his eyebrows at me. "Can we recruit this guy?" he muttered, only half joking.

I would have happily given Volkov to the MC if I could, but he wasn't under my command. From my dealings with him in the past, he had always been level-headed and had appeared to have the patience of a saint. Like this, the man was a loose cannon. Unpredictable and a liability if I couldn't keep him in check.

Even so, I had to admit, when he was like this he had his advantages.

"He's not here," Fontana finally screamed. "Jr went to Chicago last night after he took the girl."

"Fuck," Cristiano muttered half under his breath and raked his hands through his hair.

His agitation set off warning bells in my head and I turned to face him. "What?"

My friend's face was just as white as Fontana's now. "I sent Victoria to the house in Chicago with Anya. She said she needed to get away for a little while. That she needed to think. I thought she would be safer there. That they both would."

Volkov was in front of Cristiano before I could even move. His eyes were wild and, with blood splattered across his face, he looked savage. "You sent Victoria away from me?" he roared.

Cristiano didn't even flinch, his own anger starting to boil over. "She begged me to help her. Anya thought it was a good idea too. You're fucking with my sister's head and she can't deal with your shit right now."

"Anya helped you?" The Russian stumbled back a step, as if Cristiano had punched him in the face. The man he'd been while he was torturing Fontana was gone now. For only a second I saw a flash of pain in his eyes, but he quickly turned it off again. Yelling something in Russian at his men, who almost jumped out of their skin before rushing after him, he then marched out of the warehouse.

I had other shit to deal with than to worry about Volkov's temper tantrum because his newest plaything had been taken away. Jr was in Chicago. That meant Scarlett was safe for the time being, but Victoria was another story.

"Does Vito know about this?" I knew he wouldn't do something that involved his sisters without talking to his father first. Not even Cristiano could withstand the wrath of Vito Vitucci if something happened to one of his daughters while on Cristiano's watch.

"I told him earlier. He agreed it was the best thing for her right now. Like me, he thought she would be safe in Chicago." He reached for his phone. "I need to tell De Stefano."

Dante De Stefano, Vito's underboss in Chicago. I'd been offered the job, but even back then I hadn't wanted to be too far from Scarlett. Like me, Dante wasn't blood, but Vito had always treated him like he was. Vito had always had some pipe dream about one of the twins marrying the man. I'd never taken him seriously about it though, but if he had let Victoria go to Chicago he might have an ulterior motive.

Like throwing his daughter at Dante to keep her out of Volkov's reach.

Better her than Scarlett. I liked Dante, but I wouldn't hesitate to kill him if he ever looked twice at what was mine.

"When did she leave?" From what Fontana—who was still bleeding out and moaning on the table—had said, Jr had left the night before, after hurting Scarlett. If Victoria hadn't left until that morning, Jr wouldn't know she was in the same city.

"I put them on the plane this morning around ten," Cristiano told me as he waited for Dante to pick up on the other end. "As long as she stays close to the house, she should be okay. But I want De Stefano to be alert until I get there."

The MC guys were listening intently. "Colt and Raider will go with you." Hawk wasn't offering out of the kindness of his dark heart, but Cristiano wasn't listening. Dante had finally picked up and he was barking out orders. "I'd go, but I'm not going to leave with Gracie still in the hospital."

I nodded, shooting a glance at the younger two Hannigan brothers. The MC did protection runs from California to Chicago and New York all the time, but Dante didn't get along with the MC as well as I did. "I'll make sure De Stefano knows your men will be coming."

Paco pulled my attention away from the MC and back to the job that was still left to do. "What should I do with this piece of shit?"

I popped my neck. "I got this."

Fontana whimpered, then began to pray.

Chapter 17

Scarlett

"You're where?"

I hadn't meant to shout and regretted it the second that I did. Fuck, my head was still throbbing.

Victoria had only called a moment ago and the first thing out of her mouth was, "Hey, I'm in Chicago."

Chicago.

Meanwhile I was in New York. Without my twin. It wasn't like we had to be connected at the hip or anything, but we'd never spent more than a night apart in our entire lives. Twenty-one years of always having her there to turn to when I needed to talk to someone. It wasn't about me missing her—which I did. Hell, I was just now finding out she was gone and my heart was already feeling the distance between us.

No, it was about watching out for her. I'd always been the one to ask if she'd checked her blood sugar. The one to give her a shot of insulin when she needed it, or force juice down her throat when it got too low. Who was going to do that now?

"I had to leave, Scarlett." There was a quiver in her voice that made me clench my hands into fists.

What the hell had I missed? I'd been away from her for twenty-four hours, but I got the feeling I had missed a hell of a lot. I knew she'd been at Anya's, but that was all anyone had told me. Seriously, what the fuck? I couldn't make sense of it all with my head pounding like it was. I probably should have taken one of the pain pills Papa had set beside my bed earlier when he'd asked if I was hungry, but I hated how tired they made me.

Squeezing the bridge of my nose, I blew out a frustrated breath. "Okay. You had to leave. What I want to know is why, Tor."

"I met Adrian's wife last night," she whispered.

Ah, fuck. That was seriously… Fuck.

"Did you kill her?" I wasn't asking to tease her. I needed to know if my twin was on the run. That was the only explanation I could accept for why she had left without saying goodbye to me. Why she had left without me, period. "Do I need to hide a body?"

A broken laugh filled my ear. "No. You know I would call Cristiano for something like that anyway. You have Ciro for dirty work, and I have our brother."

"That's good to know. I couldn't really hide a body right now if I wanted to." I could barely walk to the damn bathroom without tripping over my own feet because I got so dizzy. "So, what happened? Is she ugly?"

"She is probably the most beautiful woman I've ever seen. And nothing happened. Not really. She stopped by Anya's apartment unexpectedly last night. She had to pick something up for Adrian."

Again, I couldn't really understand what was so bad about all of that that it would send my sister running to another state. "Tor, sweetie, I love you. But right now I need you to break this down into an even more simpler explanation because I'm not following you. I get that seeing that douchebags wife probably stung, but you knew he was married."

"It didn't just sting," she cried. "You have no idea how much it hurt when I came face to face with that woman. She has everything I want, Scarlett. Everything. She's his wife and the mother of his child." A sob bubbled out of her. "I…I didn't just come face to face with his wife. I saw his son. That little boy looks just like him, and I… That's one thing I can never have, Scarlett. You know that. I can never have that. Never."

Now I got it. I knew what had hurt her so badly that she had run away without me.

It wasn't that Victoria *couldn't* have kids of her own, but that she *shouldn't*. Her diabetes was so severe that getting pregnant had the potential of killing her. Her kidneys were already feeling the effects of the damn disease. A baby would complicate that even more. She'd always said she wouldn't ever take the risk by trying to get pregnant, and even though she'd never really thought of boys and sex, she'd gone on the pill when she was seventeen.

Her biggest dream was to be a mother, though, and she'd talked about adopting several times over the last few years.

"I'm so sorry, Tor." My heart was breaking for her. I wanted to reach through the phone and wrap her in my arms, tell her it was all going to be okay. It wouldn't be, though. Nothing about this would ever be okay and I wouldn't lie to her, not about this.

She loved Adrian and it had been a fucking stab to the heart to see what she couldn't have.

"Me too," she whispered. "And I'm really sorry about last night. I never should have let you go to the bathroom alone. I was lost in my own little world and you got hurt."

"That wasn't your fault. It was mine. I should have been more alert. Hell, we probably shouldn't have even left the house last night." That wasn't something I was going to admit to Papa—or worse, Ciro—though. I didn't need either one of them getting a bigger head than they already had.

Especially that particular *capo*.

Now that some of the shock was starting to wear off, I realized exactly where Victoria was. Who she was with.

Dante.

An evil smile pulled at my lips as I took a perverse pleasure in knowing at least one of us would be throwing a tailspin at the arrogant ass underboss's well-ordered life. I liked Dante more than my own brother, although the same couldn't be said for Victoria. Growing up, before he'd taken over as the high and mighty underboss and moved to Chicago, I'd loved tormenting Dante. He'd even come for a few visits when we were in Sicily, although that probably had more to do with our cousin Allegra and not either of us.

Why else would he stay in the same house with a man who basically hated that he existed? My uncle Gio detested Dante, but because he was part of the *Cosa Nostra* he hadn't been able to turn down the invitation to stay at the compound in Sicily.

Papa had never made it a secret that he would like to make Dante De Stefano his son-in-law, but my stupid heart had always belonged to Ciro. His relationship with both me and my sister had always been that of a brother and sisters. Papa was just out of luck where his daughters were concerned.

"How is Dante?"

Victoria blew out a huff. "He's annoying as always. I swear, I probably should have asked to go back to Sicily rather than here. Nona is so much easier to deal with than Dante."

"Because you can wind Nona around your little finger, while Dante sees right through you," I reminded her with a small laugh, only to groan when the sound made my head hurt more.

"Whatever," she mumbled, but I was thankful to hear a touch of amusement in her voice. It was good to know Volkov hadn't completely destroyed her sense of humor even if he'd decimated her heart. "I should let you go, Scarlett. Cristiano told me you have a concussion. Please get some rest, and call me every day."

I didn't want to end our call, but my headache was only getting worse. "I promise, Tor. I love you."

"Love you back."

I didn't lower the phone until she had hung up on her end. Without her voice in my ear the room suddenly felt too big. Empty—just like a part of my heart was no. I didn't want to be so far away from my twin. It hurt worse than my headache and bruised ribs combined.

Tossing the phone aside, I turned over on the bed. Ridiculously, I was fighting tears. Stupid headache. Stupid ribs. Stupid Adrian Volkov. One spilled free as I closed my eyes and tried to turn the world off.

A shifting on the mattress pulled me out of a deep, dreamless sleep hours later. I didn't have to open my eyes to know Ciro had returned and was now getting comfortable in my bed. I bit down on my lip, once again fighting tears. It was only now hitting home that I had no control over anything.

My sister was gone. I hated Volkov for hurting her so bad that she felt like she couldn't even be in the same city with him. My body had been used as a punching bag. Santino was a mean motherfucker. Papa had told me that Jr enjoyed hurting women, that rape was his favorite sport. What a fucking pussy.

But Ciro had kept his promise and had come back to me. In the end, I realized that was all that mattered. Not even trying to hold back my tears this time, I reached for Ciro before his head had even hit the pillow. Thick, strong arms carefully enfolded me against him, his lips already pressing into my hair.

"What's wrong, *vita mia*?"

His deep voice was like a soothing caress over my frayed nerves and I sucked in a shuddery breath. "Tor is gone. I hurt all over. I'm scared. I…I missed you." It all came flooding out, but I didn't care. With Ciro I was allowed to feel all of those things. He would protect me and make everything better. He always had.

One arm released me and the lamp on my nightstand was switched on. I buried my face in his chest to shield my eyes in case the light made me nauseous. Slowly, cautiously, I lifted my head, exposing myself to it a little at a time. When the pain didn't increase and my stomach didn't protest, I let out a relieved breath. After wiping away the last of my tears with his calloused thumb, Ciro reached for the bottle of pain medication and extracted one before taking the bottle of water Papa had left earlier.

After I swallowed the pill, he turned the light off and pulled me close once again. "You have nothing to be afraid of as long as I'm breathing, *vita mia*," he promised after a few minutes of just holding me.

There in the cocoon he was wrapping me in, I felt like nothing bad could happen.

Chapter 18

Scarlett

It took over a week before the headache completely went away. My ribs weren't nearly as sore, and the bruises on my face were almost completely faded, with just a little yellow hint to them. Ciro had finally relented and let me out of bed, although I hadn't been complaining too much about being there as long as he was lying beside me.

Today he was doing something with my father and I was wandering around the house feeling lost. It was lonely without Victoria, or even Cristiano to talk to. I was almost desperate enough to talk to a few of the guards who were always walking around the house.

Almost.

Deciding that what I really needed was some fresh air, I opened the front door and nearly walked right into the wide shoulders of one of Ciro's men. I stumbled back in surprise, but his reflexes were as quick as lightning and he grasped my arms before I could fall on my ass.

"Are you okay?"

I grimaced and looked up at the man. I knew a few of Ciro's men better than Papa's. Desi wasn't as tall as Ciro or my brother, but he wasn't short by anyone's definition either. His hair was a dark brown and cut short, but it was his lips that instantly drew a person's eyes. I hadn't seen lips that beautiful on a man ever. They should have looked too feminine on him, but somehow they fit him perfectly. I doubted few men would ever mention it to him. While his lips were on the beautiful side, the rest of him screamed something completely opposite.

Mysterious and dangerous.

To me he was just Desi. I'd always liked him. He didn't ignore me like everyone else did.

"I'll live," I assured him. "Just needed a little air. I've been locked up for too damn long."

A half smile lifted at those full lips but quickly disappeared. "Do you need anything?"

"You could break me out of this place. I wouldn't mind going to visit Mary." She had come to see me several times over the last week, but I understood she couldn't do it every day. She had Felicity and the MC guys still staying at her house.

"Sorry, Miss Vitucci. *Capo* said you weren't to leave the house without him."

"Of course he did," I muttered. Ciro had told me not to go anywhere without him, but seriously, I couldn't wait around for him in order to leave the compound. Knowing there was no use in arguing with Desi since he was only following orders—and he never defied his *capo*—I stepped around him. "In that case, I guess I'll take a walk."

"Of course," he said with a nod and fell into step beside me.

"The place is surrounded by at least thirty men, Desi. I think I'm safe."

"*Capo* said to watch out for you."

I rolled my eyes but didn't argue further. I was freaking bored and it was nice to have someone I could talk to. If he didn't want to talk back that was fine, I'd just talk at him.

The warm sun felt good on my skin. I loved every season in New York, was comfortable in any weather. Winter was my favorite though, especially when it was snowing. As little girls, Victoria and I had loved making snow angels in the back yard. Then we would build a snowman family and Victoria would con Cristiano to come outside to play with us. We had an entire stash of premade snowballs just waiting on him and would ambush him as soon as he walked outside. If Ciro or Dante were with him, we made plenty of extras and would nail them all in the face.

Remembering how much fun we all used to have made me miss my sister even more and some of the pleasure of the summer heat faded. Desi wasn't much of a talker, but at least he was polite and didn't treat me like someone he was being forced to babysit—even though he was.

By the time we walked the thirty or so acres around the house and returned to the front door there were two blacked-out SUVs in the driveway.

Figuring Papa and Ciro had returned, I left Desi at the door and went back inside. I found Papa and Benito already in the living room, glasses of scotch in their hands, but no sign of Ciro.

"Did Ciro not come back with you, Papa?" I asked as I entered the room.

He gave me a teasing pout. "Why is it always Ciro you want to see and never your poor papa?" he complained.

I didn't have a ready answer for him. At least not one I would willingly give my father. He didn't need to know that I ached when I wasn't with Ciro, like part of myself was missing without him beside me. Or that all I could think about was how good it felt to sleep in his arms every night.

He especially didn't need to know I was going out of my mind with wanting Ciro because the man hadn't done more than give me short, sweet kisses. I knew he was holding back because he wanted me to get better before things went further, but he was killing me with those kisses.

Papa probably didn't want to know any of that anyway.

He shook his head at my silence. "See how it is, Ben? This one has fallen in love and can't find room in her heart to love her papa too."

Benito chucked and I didn't even try to deny it. I'd always loved Ciro and we all knew it. "I will always love you, Papa." I kissed his cheek, then stepped back, smirking. "Did he come with you or not?"

"He's upstairs," Benito said, laughing harder at Papa's crestfallen face. "Probably looking for you."

"Thanks, *Zio*," I blew him a kiss as I left the room.

"Why can't I send the boy to Chicago with everyone else?" I heard Papa grumble behind me, only partially teasing.

"You could try," Benito commented. "Not so sure you would succeed as long as that little beauty was still here."

Shaking my head at the way they were joking around, I headed for the stairs. Papa would never send Ciro away. He was the one man in the entire *Costa Nostra* who was indispensable. Even I knew that.

Upstairs, I went straight to my room, knowing that was where I was most likely to find him. Opening my bedroom door, I heard the shower running in my connecting bathroom. My mouth went dry just thinking about him in there naked, only for my panties to grow wet with need. I wanted to join him, but I wasn't nearly as brave as I acted.

Not where a naked Ciro was concerned.

I was too unsure of myself when it came to lust and sex. I knew he wanted me, and I sure as hell wanted him, but things had been going at a snail's pace with us this past week. His soft, chaste kisses were driving me crazy, but if I was really and truly honest with myself I would admit I was glad he had been taking his time with me. The only experience I had was the little he'd taught me and what I'd read in books.

There were things I wanted to do to him, things I knew men were supposed to love. Like suck his cock. *Fuck, I wanted to suck his cock so bad.* But I didn't want to embarrass myself by pretending to know things I had no clue about. What if I tried and I was clumsy? What if he didn't like how I did it?

What if I bit him?

Setting down on the end of my bed, I waited. Soon the water shut off, but he was still in the bathroom five minutes later. I started biting on my bottom lip, wondering if I should just grow a pair and go in there. What was the worst that could happen?

He'd laugh at me.

He'd tell me no.

He wouldn't want me.

The door opened and he walked out, already dressed in a pair of black dress pants and blue shirt that matched his eyes. The shirt was only buttoned halfway up, showing me a delicious view of his tan, thickly muscled chest. He smelled clean with just the hint of his subtle but intoxicating cologne. It reminded me of open skies mixed with the kind of energy only a man like this one could handle.

Seeing me sitting on the bed, he grinned, drawing my attention to his freshly shaved face. I felt a small pang of loss at his week-old beard. I'd liked his scruffiness, had enjoyed the feel of his stubble against my lips when he would kiss me. Not that I disliked him clean-shaven. Hell, no woman alive would ever think this man was less sexy for having a smooth face. The scruff was just my favorite.

"Hello, *vita mia*." He bent to kiss my cheek, enticing me with his cologne all the more. "Did you miss me today?"

"Yes." A week ago I would have lied, but not now. There was no use in trying.

Something darkened in his eyes, making my breath catch in my throat. He took my hand, pressed a kiss to my palm, then carried it to his chest. "Help me with this tie, would you?"

I stood and took the tie I had only just then noticed hanging from his other hand. It was a darker blue than his eyes, but I loved how it made them stand out even more. This close to him, I had to concentrate hard on the task at hand. The feel of his hard chest under my fingertips, the heat that seemed to radiate off him and burn into me was a mixture that made me lightheaded.

Clearing my throat, I was finally able to get his tie perfect and took a much needed step back so I could think again. "You look really good. Do you have a meeting?"

"Nope." He caught my hand and guided me over to the closet. "I have a date."

My head jerked back, pain slicing through me for a moment before my jealous brain caught up and I realized what he was really saying. Opening the double door to the massive closet, he started shifting through the entire wall of elegant dresses Victoria had tirelessly collected for me.

"A-a date?" I stuttered.

I'd never been on a date before. Ever. Guys were too afraid of my father, brother…even Ciro, to ask me out. Not that I would have ever accepted if they had. From the time I was eleven, it had only been Ciro for me.

It would only ever be him for me.

Finding a metallic blue that complemented his shirt, he pulled it off the hanger and tossed it over his shoulder before grabbing a pair of heels that I would probably break my neck in. Satisfied with what he'd come up with, he pulled me out of the closet and into the bathroom. "Shower. Do whatever it is you do. Then come downstairs when you're done." He glanced at his watch, seeming distracted. "I made reservations for seven, so don't rush."

"Wait." My head was spinning. He was taking me on a date? I felt oddly giddy and it was taking everything inside me not to start giggling like a nervous fifteen-year-old being asked to the mall for a slice of pizza. This was all new territory for me.

Ciro turned those amazing blue eyes on me, his face full of concern and something else. Doubt? No, it couldn't be that. Ciro was not the kind of guy to doubt anything he did. "What's wrong? Do you not want to go to dinner with me?"

I shook my head and his face seemed to drop. "No, no—I want to go," I rushed to assure him and he actually breathed a sigh of relief. "I'm just… I don't…" I cut off my flow of unfinished sentences and bit into my lip. "I've never been on a date before," I whispered.

Hunger filled his eyes and he sucked in a harsh breath. "Me either, *vita mia*. We get to share this first together." He bent his head and kissed my cheek. "And many, many more." His deep voice rumbled in my ear, making me tremble.

Instinctively I reached out, steadying myself by clutching at his shirt. "Ciro."

I felt his tongue touch the delicate skin under my ear. "I've changed my mind. Hurry, Scarlett. Get dressed as fast as you can, because I don't trust myself not to make love to you right here, right now." He stepped back before I could beg him to do just that. His jaw tense, his eyes bright with desire, he gritted out a simple, "Hurry," then turned and left me there, shivering with suppressed need that left my knees weak.

Chapter 19

Ciro

I was shaking like a boy. It was a new experience for me. Fuck, no one had ever made me this weak before. Except for Scarlett.

I wanted to do this right, wanted to show her all the things I would always give her before I took something precious from her. I had to show her tonight, because I knew I wouldn't last another day. Hell, I wouldn't last to the end of the night.

It had taken every ounce of willpower I possessed not to take things further over the past week. Watching as her bruises had slowly faded had been torture. Every second had been worth it, though. Every. Second. Sleeping with her in my arms. Waking up to her beautiful face each morning. Having her pout when I woke her up too early and had to leave her.

She'd been showing me what she would always give me. Peace. Love. Her.

That was all I'd ever wanted.

I waited for her downstairs while she got ready. I hadn't been lying when I told her that I'd never been on a date before either. I was twenty-six and had never taken a woman out. The women I'd fucked around with in the past were not the kind a man took out to dinner. There hadn't been many of them in the past few years. Just the random hookup when I needed to blow off steam. This was new territory for me, but I was glad I was exploring it with Scarlett.

"Relax, boy," Vito said with a grin as I paced back and forth in front of the unlit fireplace while he and my father slowly drank his supply of well-aged scotch. "You'll only make yourself gray."

"Scarlett doesn't twiddle around getting ready, son," my father said with a grin. "She won't keep you waiting like your mother does me."

I didn't answer either one of them. My pacing had nothing to do with Scarlett taking her time to get ready. It was so I could burn off some of the excess energy that was already flooding off me in waves. If I didn't work some of it off, I was going to climb those stairs again and fuck her in the goddamn bathroom right now.

"Why do I feel like I'm losing my baby, Ben?" Vito muttered.

"I don't think of it as losing your baby. More like me gaining a daughter."

"That doesn't make me feel better."

I ignored them, knowing they were just messing with each other and trying to get under my skin. They weren't even close to doing that. Scarlett would be my wife one day. I relished taking Vito's baby away from him and giving my father the daughter he and my mother had always wanted.

"Well? How do I look?"

All three of our heads snapped around at the soft voice behind me. My breath caught in my throat, my heart actually stopping for two full beats before kick-starting almost painfully. No, it wasn't pain. It was exhilaration. This beautiful woman was mine.

She'd left her hair down, but she'd done something to it to make it fall in soft waves around her face. Her makeup was minimal, highlighting her eyes in a mysterious way and enhancing her luscious lips. The dress fell to her knees, but it seemed to fuse to every curve like a second skin. With the heels, her legs looked like they went on for miles. I wanted to kiss every inch of bare skin. Wanted those damn legs wrapped around my waist.

While I stood there, stupefied by the sheer beauty before me, the other two men stood and enfolded her in hugs. "You look beautiful, *passerotta*."

"Thank you, Papa." She stepped back from her father, smiled sweetly at my father, then turned her eyes on me. When our gazes locked, the entire room seemed to disappear. All I saw was her. "Will I do?"

For the first time in my life I was speechless. I opened my mouth to tell her I'd never seen anything so breathtakingly beautiful in my life, but no words would come. A slow grin teased at her lips. "I'll take that as a yes."

"Close your mouth, son," my father muttered as he passed me on the way back to his chair. "You're drooling, boy."

My mouth snapped closed and I had to shake my head a few times to get some sense of control over myself. "Ready?" My voice came out hoarse and weak.

Her grin grew bigger. "I'm ready," she murmured in a soft, husky voice that sent a shot of pure need straight to my dick.

Vito touched her shoulder and she hugged him again. "Have fun, *passerotta*."

Outside, I helped her into the back of the SUV where Desi was already sitting behind the wheel with Paco beside him in the passenger seat. Scarlett scooted across the back seat, letting me in beside her. As I climbed in, I reached for her hand, keeping her from going too far.

"Let's go," I told Desi.

"Where are we going?" Scarlett asked after a few minutes.

I shifted with difficulty to face her better. Even in the huge SUV, I had little leg room. "Just a little Italian place I know."

She rolled her eyes, but the smile on her face hadn't faltered. "So, like one of about two hundred or so restaurants. That narrows it down."

"Smartass." I lifted her hand and pressed a kiss to her knuckles. The way her breath seemed to come in little pants at that innocent caress made my dick thicken and dig into the zipper on my pants. "It's a place that holds good memories for us, *vita mia*."

The sun was still out, letting me see the way her brown eyes lit up. "Don Rubirosa's?" I winked, and her even white teeth bit into her glossy bottom lip, those brown eyes darkening. "We ate there together before I went to Sicily."

I nodded. "We did."

Her chin started to tremble but she quickly forced it to stop. "Are you going to send me away again? Is that what this is about?"

I leaned closer so I could speak into her ear, not because I didn't want my men to hear, but so I could taste her neck. I traced a circle just under her lobe with my tongue. "No, baby. That's not ever going to happen again. This is more. So much more." She shivered, leaning into me, arching her neck in a silent demand for more. I pressed a kiss against her skin. "Just be patient and I promise we will talk over dinner."

She leaned against me weakly. "Ciro, I don't think I'm strong enough to handle it if you push me away again," she whispered.

"I swear on my life that will never happen, *vita mia*." I'd given up on fighting what I felt for her. If I pushed her away now, I might as well put a bullet through my head because I would be dead without her.

She didn't reply. Kissing her again, I tucked her close. She still didn't completely trust me, and I couldn't blame her. It would take time to make her see that I was done hurting us both.

Don Rubirosa's was the best Italian restaurant in the entire country. People willingly waited for hours at a time just for a table. It was also run by the

Cosa Nostra. I could have shown up and been given a table immediately with no issue, but tonight I'd made a reservation, wanting everything to be perfect for Scarlett.

Desi pulled up in front of the restaurant. Paco stepped out and opened the door for Scarlett while I came around the back. Once I had her hand in mine, he climbed back into the SUV and Desi drove away. Scarlett shifted on her feet unsteadily for a moment, her dislike of heels showing in her eyes for a moment until she was able to stand with confidence.

I clasped her elbows and bent my head until my lips touched her forehead. "You look beautiful."

"You look pretty good yourself." She tilted her head to the side, assessing me with a critical eye. Lifting her hands, she straightened my tie and then smirked. "Perfect."

Inside, the place was overflowing with people waiting for a table. The smells of fresh pasta, garlic and tomatoes filled my senses. I heard Scarlett actually moan with pleasure at the scents. Keeping her close, I approached the hostess. The girl's eyes widened when she saw me coming.

"Mr. Donati," she said with a smile. "Your table is ready, sir." She grabbed a wine menu. "This way."

Behind us the people still waiting were noticeably quiet. Several of them knew who I was, even fewer of them knew Scarlett's identity. None of them had the balls to approach me. As we walked through the restaurant, people stopped eating to watch us. This happened every time I ate here, I was used to it, but I knew it made Scarlett uncomfortable.

My usual table was at the back of the restaurant, so I could see everyone but few could actually see me. I seated Scarlett, then took the chair beside her so I could keep her close. The hostess handed over the wine list, promised our server would be right with us, then turned and walked back to her post.

Leaning forward, Scarlett snatched the list from my fingers. "Primitivo or sangrivese?"

I leaned back in my chair, watching her with pleasure. "Whichever you prefer, *vita mia.* I want you to have whatever makes you happy."

Slowly her eyes lifted from the list. "Being with you makes me happy, Ciro. It's all I've ever really wanted."

I took her left hand, brought it to my lips. "It's the same for me," I told her with complete honesty. "I'm an idiot for pushing you away for so many years, Scarlett, but trust me when I say it hurt me just as much as it hurt you when you got on that plane three years ago." Part of me had gone with her, and it was only when I'd seen her again that I had finally felt whole once more.

The waiter appeared. He wasn't the usual guy I dealt with, but I didn't question it. Rubirosa wasn't an idiot. He wasn't going to hire anyone who even smelled like one of our rivals. "A bottle of primitivo," I told the guy, knowing it was exactly what she wanted. "The spaghetti bolognese for her."

I heard a soft huff leave her and shot her a smirk. She shook her head, making her hair fall forward. "He'll have the penne with the arrabbiata sauce," she told the waiter, but her eyes were glued to my face. "Heavy on the arrabbiata or he will probably send it back."

"Good choices."

We didn't even spare him another look, too lost in each other's eyes to care. She knew me better than anyone on the planet. Better than my mother, my best friend—better than I even knew myself at times. It had scared me once upon a time, now it just made me glad that she hadn't given up on me. On us.

The waiter left and I leaned forward, pushing her hair back from her face. The silky tresses clung to my fingers, the look in her eyes daring me to come closer, her lips begging to be kissed. I gave her what she wanted, savoring the taste of her lip gloss for a moment before forcing myself to pull away.

Her lashes lifted after a moment, her lips slightly swollen from our kiss. "Those are becoming addicting."

"Becoming?" I shook my head. "No, *vita mia*. They already are."

The waiter returned with the bottle of wine. He poured me a small sample, I tasted it, then I gave a nod of approval before he poured us both a glass of the red wine. After he left again, Scarlett sat quietly in her chair, making me wonder what was on her mind.

"Talk to me," I urged, wanting to hear her voice.

She smiled. "What would you like to talk about?"

I shrugged. "Anything. Nothing. Whatever you want."

She picked up her wine glass, took a small sip, then a larger swallow. "Did my father tell you he called me into his office this morning?"

I stiffened. "No," I gritted out, dread filling my chest. "He didn't mention it."

"He asked me the craziest question, and then I remembered something you said to me when I was in the hospital and it all made a weird kind of sense." She took another sip, then put her glass down. I clenched my hands on the table, waiting for her answer, dreading it. "I told him no, Ciro. As pissed as I am at Santino for what happened to me, I have better things to think about than daydreaming about how I might kill him if given the chance."

Hell. I'd been holding my breath, waiting on Vito to offer his daughter the option of killing Jr herself. I'd thought she was too much of a little hothead to turn him down, but fuck, I was glad that I'd been wrong.

I lifted a hand, cupped her cheek. "Thank you. You don't know how relieved I am right now."

She turned her head, pressing her lips into my palm. "Don't thank me. I just don't care enough to want to be the one to put a bullet in him. I'd much rather save it for Volkov." Her eyes narrowed as she thought about the Russian. "Can you arrange that?"

"Afraid not, baby. For all his faults, the guy comes in handy at times." I winked when she only glowered at me. "One day you'll thank me for keeping him alive."

"Doubtful," she muttered, reaching for her wine again.

The waiter brought us salad and breadsticks. She picked at the fresh tomatoes and basil salad topped with thickly sliced mozzarella, lost in her own thoughts. I knew she was missing her sister and her dislike of Volkov grew more and more every day she and Victoria were apart. I hated seeing her so lost without her other half, but in the long run, I knew it would be good for both sisters to have a little time apart. Especially for Victoria, who Cristiano had confided in me was slowly drawing into herself. Apparently the happy twin was no longer the carefree butterfly she'd always been. Now she was moody and distant.

The food arrived moments later and her angry pout was replaced with a sigh of pure bliss as she dug into her favorite meal. I barely tasted the spicy arrabbiata as I watched her enjoy her food. Those happy little moans that she probably wasn't even aware she was making as she dipped a breadstick into her sauce went straight to my dick.

Only when she'd had her fill did she speak to me again. Wiping her mouth, she asked the question I'd promised her an answer to earlier. "If this date isn't about sending me away, then tell me what it really is about."

I took her hand, stroked my thumb over her fingers, keeping my eyes locked on hers. "It's about new beginnings. Our new beginning, *vita mia.*

Tonight you are mine and I'm yours. This date is only the start of our lives together."

Her face softened. "Ciro—"

I leaned forward, brushed a soft kiss over her lips to stop whatever she might have said. "We were made for each other and I was too stupid to accept that. I will give you the world, Scarlett. Whatever you want. Whatever you need. Because you are my life."

Tears filled her eyes, gutting me. "That sounds oddly close to a marriage proposal," she whispered.

"It is." I reached into my pants pocket and pulled out the little box that had been weighing me down all day. I'd wanted to wait for this part after we'd had dessert, but I couldn't. I'd waited too long already. Setting it on the table, I watched her face as she looked down at it. She swallowed hard, the pulse at the base of her throat racing like a bullet train, mimicking my own. "I've wasted years of our lives. I won't waste another minute. Be my wife."

I sucked in a harsh breath when she just continued to stare at the little black box, not so much as blinking. I hadn't been nervous about doing this because I knew it was the only path for us. I hadn't sweat buckets when I'd told her father what I had planned for her tonight. I hadn't freaked out wondering if she would say yes or not when I'd picked up the ring inside that damn little box she was so focused on right then. No, it was right now, right that very second, that the doubts and the nerves were starting to eat at my sanity.

"Fuck, Scarlett, please say you'll marry me." I had never begged for anything in my life until right then and there. I didn't care who saw or heard. I would fall at her feet and beg with everything inside of me if that was what she wanted.

Her head shot up then, the smallest smile teasing at her lips, but she was shaking her head. "You left out three words, Ciro."

I tightened my hold on her fingers, my heart trying to beat right out of my chest. What? Three words? Three…words. I closed my eyes and pressed my forehead against hers. "I love you. I always have. I always will. In this life and the next."

"That's more than three words," she softly chided.

My heart was going to explode if she didn't give me an answer. "Scarlett, I will get on my knees right here and now if that's what you want. Just please, say yes."

She pulled back until her brown eyes met mine. "Yes, Ciro. I'll marry you."

A lump filled my throat, cutting off my ability to breathe for a moment. That look in her eyes that said without words she loved me, that soft smile on her lips as she said 'yes' again and then again. She was all I'd ever wanted and she was giving herself completely over to me in that moment.

Chapter 20

Scarlett

I felt like I was in the middle of a dream. The best dream of my life, but still a dream.

From the minute we'd walked through the door of Don Rubirosa's, everything around me seemed to slow down. The way people turned their heads to watch us walk by, the way the entire restaurant had grown quiet until I was sure no one but me and Ciro were actually breathing. When he'd pulled out my chair and scooted me in, his fingers lingering on my back for only a moment—that moment had lasted an eternity and was over far too soon.

Drinking wine with him.

Eating.

Talking like we'd always done.

And then…

My gaze kept going back to the little box that was still sitting unopened between us on the table. First dates didn't normally end in a marriage proposal; I was fairly sure of that even if it was the only one I'd ever been on. Then again, there was nothing normal about either one of us, not to mention our relationship.

"I love you. I always have. I always will. In this life and the next."

Those words floated through my head, filling my entire body with a heat that threatened to consume me. I felt like I'd been waiting for those words for an eternity, had feared I'd never have them from this beast of a man. Yet he'd given them to me freely, with the kind of quiet appeal that had pulled at my heart until I'd been powerless to give him any other answer but the one we were both so desperate for me to breathe.

"Yes," I told him again for the fourth—or was it the fifth?—time.

I pulled my eyes away from the box to watch him. He swallowed hard, his throat seeming to convulse for a single heartbeat and then he was sucking in a breath that sounded relieved. Had he doubted me? Was he scared I would say no?

He snatched up the box, the little thing completely disappearing in his huge paw of a hand. With fingers that shook he opened the top, but I wasn't interested in what the ring looked like. It could have been one of those silly plastic rings kids got out of a cereal box and I would have worn it with pride. The only thing I cared about was that it had come from Ciro and it meant I was his.

Forever.

Long, thick fingers pulled out the ring. Tossing the box back onto the table, he grasped my left hand gently, as if he was afraid he would hurt me if he didn't do this just right. My eyes stayed on his face as he concentrated on putting his ring in place on my finger. The metal of the ring felt cool against my skin, but his heat quickly soaked into it, burning me. Blue eyes were over-bright with emotion, his throat still bobbing up and down. When the ring was finally perfectly in place, he lifted it to his lips.

"I swear to you, *vita mia*, you will never regret this. Never. I will love you like no man has ever loved any woman." His voice was low and raspy. Raw with all the emotions trying to fight their way past his iron-tight control.

I reached for him, cupping his face in both of my hands, not caring who saw as I leaned forward and kissed him. It was the first time I'd ever kissed him first, the first time I'd ever just taken what I wanted. His breathing changed as soon as my lips skimmed over his, his big hands grasping my wrists but I didn't pull my hands away. I kept the kiss soft, light, but when I pulled back we were both desperate for air.

Ciro leaned his forehead against mine. I loved when he did that. I felt like he was blocking out everything but the two of us, that in those brief moments like this we were the only people on the planet. "I love you," he said in a husky voice.

"I love you, Ciro."

His big body jerked like he'd been stabbed and in the next moment he was on his feet. The look on his face was wild and had my heart going crazy in my chest at the hunger I saw in those blue eyes I loved. He reached for his wallet, threw a handful of bills on the table, then took my hand and pulled me to my feet. Ciro's steps were long and quick and I had to practically run in my heels to keep up with him. My left hand was tucked in his, and I was actually laughing by the time we reached the door.

Outside, on the sidewalk, he turned around so fast I would have fallen if he hadn't had such a tight hold on my hand. He jerked me against his hard body, his head lowering even before I'd pressed myself against him. I tasted the wine and the spicy arrabbiata on his breath and moaned as his tongue invaded my mouth, those two flavors mixing with his own unique taste. Everything faded around us. The noise of the New York City traffic, the people walking up and down the busy sidewalk, the lights of all the surrounding buildings. All I could hear, see, feel and taste was Ciro.

This kiss was different from every one of the kisses he'd given me before. There was no tenderness in this one, no contained passion. He was letting it all go, letting it burn and brand me. I loved it, savored it, silently begged for more. His left hand went to my hip, his fingers squeezing my ass and pulling my lower body roughly closer. His right hand thrust into my hair, cupping the back of my head as he angled me just the way he wanted and promising me he wouldn't let go.

My hands went to his chest, fisting the soft material of his shirt, making my own promises of keeping him forever. I felt his lower body hardening more and more with each passing second, felt his dick flex against my lower stomach and I squirmed against him, seeking closer contact. I was on fire for him, my panties beyond soaked and my desire was now coating the inside of my thighs.

He could have pushed me up against the window of the building behind me and fucked me then and there and I would have begged for more. I was so lost in our kiss, the feel of his hands on me that I wouldn't have cared who saw us.

The hand on my ass squeezed hard and he lifted his head. I was gasping for air, trying to suck in as much life-giving oxygen as I could before he kissed me again. But when he lowered his head it was to brush a butterfly-soft kiss over the tip of my nose. "I need you in a bed. Right now."

I licked my lips, savoring the taste of him there. "Yes," I whispered. "Yes. Hurry."

"Fuck," he growled, stealing a short, hard kiss and then he moved toward the street.

When he reached for the door of a SUV I was surprised to find it was the one we'd arrived in. Desi was already behind the wheel, with Paco right beside him. Neither looked at us, and I was too lost in the euphoria of that kiss to care if they had seen us or not.

"Drop us off at my apartment," Ciro ordered.

Desi nodded but didn't say so much as a word as he did a U-turn and headed for Ciro's place. Ciro turned his body toward me, one huge hand cupping my hip, the other pulling my head onto his chest. I could hear how erratically his heart was beating and delighted that it matched my own. On the fifteen-minute drive he didn't try to kiss me again, didn't so much as move, and I knew he was holding on to his control with difficulty.

Knowing that I could do that to him, make this big powerful man have to fight for control, was exhilarating.

Desi pulled to a stop outside of a high-rise and Ciro jumped out. Taking my hand, he practically pulled me from the vehicle and onto the street. I'd never been to his apartment before but my curiosity about what it would look like was nonexistent as he used a keycard to open the lobby door and then activate the elevators.

There were two men in suits sitting behind a desk beside the elevators and as we passed them, I saw each give Ciro a single nod in greeting. Even in my desire-fogged mind I knew this entire building was *Cosa Nostra* protected. I wondered who else lived there, but that thought was quickly pushed straight out of my head as Ciro stepped into the elevator.

He dropped my hand and with an animalistic growl bent until he had my ass in both his hands, lifting me up like I weighed nothing at all. I gasped and wrapped my legs around his waist. His head lowered, his face burying in the small bit of cleavage the dress offered. I could feel his hardness straining for freedom, flexing against my inner left thigh. I squirmed against him, wanting to feel that hardness rubbing against my damp folds.

Ciro kissed the tops of my breast, his tongue swirling little circles in the valley between them. My dress was inching up until his fingers were touching the undersides of my ass cheeks. My fingers stroked over his short hair, down his neck and into the collar of his shirt. His skin was scalding to the touch but I craved the burn.

All too soon the elevator was opening again. Ciro lifted his head for only a second and I realized we were actually outside his apartment. I hadn't even felt the elevator move. Tightening his hold on my ass, he walked with me against him like that to the door. He didn't pull out the key card he'd used to activate the elevator. His hand pressed against a key pad beside the door and after a moment it beeped and I heard the door unlock with a soft click.

Letting go of my ass long enough to open the door, he nudged it open with his foot and then walked in. With each step he took his hardness rubbed against my wetness, making me moan as pleasure so intense it made me see stars shot through my entire body. Once we were over the threshold, he kicked it closed and then pressed me against the cool wood.

"When?"

He was kissing up and down my neck, so his growl-like question made no sense to me. "When…what?" I whimpered when his teeth grazed across my earlobe and then down my neck to bite into my shoulder.

"When will you marry me?" he demanded without lifting his head.

His teeth sank deeper into the flesh of my shoulder and he started to suck. Holy shit, that felt good. I couldn't think, couldn't fucking breathe, because whatever he was doing was too much and yet not enough. Never enough.

"Scarlett." He released my flesh and lifted his head until our eyes were locked. The need that was glaring back at me made me shiver. "When will you marry me? I need to know. Now."

"Wh-whenever you want. I don't care. I don't. All I've ever wanted was you. Nothing else matters." The truth poured out of me and his hands tightened almost painfully on my ass. Why did that feel so good? It should have hurt, but it only made me that much more desperate for him.

"Soon," he growled. "Say you'll marry me soon."

"Soon," I promised. "Tomorrow. Next week. Whenever you want. *Ti amo tanto. Voglio passare il resto della mia vita con te.*" The words flowed off my tongue and I didn't even realize I wasn't speaking English anymore.

I love you so much.

I want to spend the rest of my life with you.

I felt him shudder, heard the change in his already uneven breathing even as his eyes darkened. "*Non posso vivere senza di te. Sei tutta per me.*"

He rarely spoke in Italian, so when he did now I savored each and every word. Tears filled my eyes as they invaded my heart. *I can't live without you. You're everything to me.* "Ciro."

"Two weeks," he whispered and lowered his head slowly this time, kissing me tenderly. "Marry me in two weeks."

"Yes," I whispered against his lips. "Two weeks." I had no idea how we would get married that fast and it didn't matter. I'd fly to Vegas and get married by one of those damn Elvis impersonators if that was what it took. I didn't need some huge wedding that cost half a million dollars. A white dress meant nothing to me. As long as he was mine and I was his, nothing else mattered to me.

Nothing.

Ciro was done being gentle. His fingers dug into my ass, grinding me against his erection. *Fuck, that feels so good.* My head fell against the door, my eyes nearly rolling back in my head as I clutched at his shoulders, trying to hold on as he drove me crazy with a need that was consuming me.

His lips touched the base of my throat, his tongue flicking over the erratic pulse that was fluttering like a hummingbird's wings. I couldn't think, couldn't breathe, from all the pleasure. I had everything I'd ever wanted right here. Nothing and no one could have fucked up my happiness in that moment.

"Bed." He growled against my throat. "We need a bed."

Bed? Hell, he could take anything he wanted from me right there against the door. But I didn't protest when his grip on my ass tightened almost painfully and he carried me across his living room. I didn't check out his decor as he made the quick trip to his bedroom. He could have had a torture rack and a dead body lying around, for all I knew.

My eyes were glued to his face. His blue eyes were wild and animalistic in a way that made me rub against his hardness as he opened the door to his bedroom. His face was set in tense lines that would have probably scared the piss out of his men.

Knowing that I had put that look on his face, knowing that I had the power to make him turn into a mindless beast, sent a thrill down my spine.

Ciro loves me.

Ciro wants me.

Ciro is going to marry me.

Those three facts kept echoing through my head until I began to shake with happiness.

Chapter 21

Scarlett

Ciro stopped abruptly and suddenly I was falling. My back hit a plush mattress. The cool silkiness of the comforter, felt delicious against my overheated arms and legs. I lifted my eyes, watched as Ciro kicked off his shoes and then reached for his belt. My eyes lingered on the large bulge that was trying to fight its way to freedom. My mouth went dry as my pussy clenched with anticipation.

The belt went flying across the room, but Ciro didn't undo his pants. He dropped to his knees in front of me, his big hands already gliding up my dress until they reached my neck. His thumb stroked over my chin until it reached my lips. I licked him, watched as his nostrils flared and he inhaled sharply.

"I want you naked. Now." He stood, his hands already full of my dress hem. I sat up long enough for him to pull it over my head, then fell back against the mattress once again. The cool air from the air-conditioning, the silky coolness of the covers, they were no relief from the heat of Ciro's gaze as he ran his eyes over my near nakedness.

I had on one of the hundreds of matching bra-and-panty sets that Victoria always bought me when she was shopping. For the first time I was glad she had a secret addiction to sexy underwear. With the way Ciro was eating up the sight of me in my sheer ice-blue bra and matching bikini panties, I mentally made a note of thanking my sister the next time she called.

The mattress depressed on either side of me as Ciro put his hands on the bed and leaned forward. His lips touched my cheek, then moved down to my jaw. I heard him breathe in deeply, his lips and nose tickling as he kissed a trail down my neck, over my collar bone and to my left shoulder. I felt the nip of his teeth as he lifted my bra strap and pulled it down my arm. Gooseflesh popped up all over my skin as I watched his head move, felt the tender bite of his teeth and warm moistness of his lips.

With my left strap halfway down my arm, he kissed his way back to my collar bone and then over to the other strap. I was trembling by the time he had it down my arm. His knees hit the mattress, making me sink into the bed more. He didn't put his weight on me, although I could feel his dick flexing against my stomach as he leaned forward to kiss me.

I kissed him back hungrily, my tongue tangling with his. I was getting drunk on his taste. The world could have ended but neither one of us would have noticed. Ciro sucked my bottom lip into his mouth roughly, and I felt the tingle from that roughness all the way to my pussy. He was stealing all the oxygen from my lungs, but I didn't need air right then.

I barely noticed him shift, was too lost in everything he was making me feel to even care what he was doing with his hands until I felt them on my breasts. I arched into his touch, seeking more even as he sucked harder on my lip. His rough fingers traced over each globe until they reached the front clasp. With the twist of his fingers the bra fell apart, exposing my aching nipples to the cool air.

Those rough fingers found my diamond-hard nipples, tracing around them teasingly. I pulled back from the kiss, crying out from the exquisite pleasure that made my body feel like there was a fireworks show going off deep inside. I gasped, sucking in deep breaths as he lowered his head, replacing his fingers with his lips.

My fingers went to his head, holding him against me. "Yes," I whimpered as he sucked my nipple against the roof of his mouth hard. "Ah, yes. More. Please, Ciro. More."

He switched from one breast to the other, showing it just as much attention. It was too much. It wasn't nearly enough. It was perfect and crazy and all I wanted was for him to make me stop aching, yet I never wanted the ache to end. It wasn't until he lifted his head that I realized I'd actually said all of those things aloud. He was helpless to put up the mask he normally hid everything he was thinking behind. I saw the need, the love, and even the awe.

Ciro's breath was shaky as he wrapped his hands around my waist and rolled onto his back, taking me with him. I landed across his chest, my hair spread out around us like a curtain. "If you don't take charge I'm going to end up hurting you," his deep voice rumbled. "You're in control here, Scarlett."

For the first time since he'd kissed me outside Don Rubirosa's, I was nervous. What if I did something he didn't like? What if he hated how I touched him? What if—?

The millions of doubts and 'what ifs' were quickly pushed to the back of my mind when Ciro skimmed his lips over mine in a kiss that stole all thoughts from my head and made my body melt against his. "Just do what feels good for you, *vita mia*," he murmured against my lips, having read my thoughts so clearly. "I'll love anything and everything you do. Don't be scared. I will never hurt or embarrass you. Trust me."

Taking my hands, he guided them to the top button of his shirt. "I'm as much yours as you are mine. Show me you know that."

Those words gave me the courage I needed to put my nervousness aside and just let myself enjoy the man underneath me. My fingers trembled as I unbuttoned each one, exposing more and more of his delicious chest to my hungry eyes. It wasn't nerves that had me quaking though, it was need that was making my blood burn through my veins.

Ciro just lay there, not daring to move, barely even breathing as I pushed the shirt apart. I could feel his eyes on me as I traced my index finger over every hard ridge and groove of his chest and abdomen. We both sucked in a deep breath when I reached the top of his pants and carefully undid the button. My fingers worked slowly and carefully over the zipper, his breath hissing out through his teeth as I stroked over the steel-like bulge.

The zipper was undone and he was breathing like he'd just run five miles without stopping, but he still didn't move. Didn't try to touch me. He didn't say a word as I tugged his pants down, exposing his black boxer briefs that stretched across his thick thighs. My fingers dipped into the top of the boxers, taking them off as I pulled his pants down. As I moved, my hair brushed over his chest, down his stomach and over his pelvis. His body seemed to jerk like he'd been electrocuted, his hands reaching out and fisting in the comforter to keep from touching me.

I finished stripping him and then sat back on my heels, drinking in the sight of him. I loved his body. The way every single muscle seemed to ripple with each breath he took. The way his olive complexion stood out especially when my much lighter skin was so close to his. One of his thighs alone was as big as I was, making me realize how small I really was. How fragile I was compared to his strength. A strength he would never use against me.

I tossed my bra aside and then reached for my panties, needing to be just as bare as he was. The hands already fisted in the comforter tightened and I shot him a smirk, knowing it was killing him not to touch me.

"You are so fucking beautiful, *vita mia.* You have no idea what you do to me."

I glanced at his long, thick erection. Blue veins had popped out along the entire length, the pink head damp with his pre-cum. "I can take a guess."

"I'm dying for you," he groaned when I just continued to look at his cock. "Come here, baby. Let me kiss you."

I went willingly. As my body pressed into his, I realized that despite our differences we fit perfectly together. His hardness against my softness was delicious. The way his heartbeat drummed against my breasts as I fell onto his chest matched the rhythm of my own. He kept his hands fisted in the covers, but his kiss was just as commanding, binding me to him just as forcefully as if he were physically holding me against him.

Ciro

Don't touch her.

I knew if I let myself so much as brush my fingertips over her soft skin I would lose all control. There would be no stopping me from taking her without first getting her ready enough to take my cock. She was too small, too innocent, and I would never cause her physical pain, not even at the expense of my own pleasure. So I kept my hands locked in the comforter.

Her soft body pressed down on mine, holding me in place with nothing more than her scent and warmth. Her lips were just as hungry as mine as she kissed me, her tongue tangling with mine. Lower, she shifted her hips back and forth, rubbing the apex of her thighs against my hard-as-stone cock. I could feel the dampness from her arousal coating us both and it was sweet torture to my throbbing body.

The moans and whimpers coming from her were driving me crazy. The way she rubbed against me like a cat wanting to be petted making my blood burn like molten lava through my veins. She had complete control this time, but I was dying for when I could have her the way I'd always dreamed. Lying beneath me. Giving me everything she had and begging for more.

Her head lifted, her lips swollen and slightly bruised from our kisses. I could see the uncertainty still lingering in her eyes. My little innocent wasn't sure what to do next, but she was enjoying every second of being in control. "Tell me what you want, Scarlett. Tell me and I'll make it a reality."

Her lashes lowered, but not before I saw the pleasure my promise had caused. "I want you to touch me." She reached for one of my hands, her fingers brushing over my clenched fist until I unfolded it and entwined them together with hers. Pulling our joined hand toward us, she rubbed it down her side until she reached her hip. She turned onto her side, half on me and half on the bed. "Touch me here," she commanded as she rubbed the back of my hand over her damp folds.

I clenched my right hand, holding the comforter tighter until I was sure I was going to crack my knuckles, but the hand she was holding touched her with tenderness. I gently released her hand and parted her drenched pussy lips, my thumb seeking out her clit. I watched her face, saw how her eyes nearly rolled back into her beautiful head as I brushed a butterfly-soft touch over the small bundle of nerves.

The way she responded to me, the way she melted and gasped my name, it was all a rush I'd never experienced before with any woman. Scarlett rolled onto her back, spreading her thighs welcomingly for me. I felt her trembling, making my own body shake in response. I continued to softly tease her clit with my thumb while I dipped into her tight little body with my middle finger.

"More," she moaned. "Mm, more."

My right hand was going numb from how hard I had it clenched, but I forgot all about it as I took my time. I memorized the feel of her petal-like clit, breathing in the scent of her sweet nectar as she grew more and more wet with each dip of my finger into that tight little pussy. Her muscles tightened around my finger, begging for more even as she pleaded for it in my ear.

She was panting, her tits practically bouncing with how fast she was breathing. Her trembling limbs were starting to tighten, her inner muscles already beginning to contract as her release grew near. I turned my head, seeking her lips. She gave them to me willingly.

Scarlett's mouth opened just enough for me to slip my tongue inside. As I stroked my tongue over hers, I pressed down on her clit and thrust a second finger into her opening. Her back arched, pushing her hips completely off the bed as her body instinctively moved against my hand, riding out her orgasm. She cried out into my mouth, but I didn't release her lips.

I swallowed every moan and whimper, every pitiful cry of my name while my hand continued to stroke her. Slowly, her body began to go languid and her hips fell back onto the bed. I rubbed her clit in gentle little circles, leaving her lips in search of her nipples. As I sucked one into my mouth, she moaned in need again.

"What do you want now, *vita mia*?" I murmured against her flesh. "Tell me."

"You," she gasped, her hips thrusting in time to my fingers still inside of her, twisting and stretching, preparing her so she could accommodate my thickness better. "Please, Ciro. I ache for you." I slipped my fingers from her tightness, making her cry out in protest. "No."

"You can't have me and my fingers, *vita mia*." I unclenched my right hand and grasped her ass with both hands, pulling her on top of me.

Fuck, I love her ass. Second only to her legs.

My thumbs caressed down the seam of her ass, making her whimper in a mixture of need and confusion. I watched her eyes, knew she loved what I'd just done but she was unsure if she was supposed to like it or not. One day, I'd make sure she knew that she could have anything and everything that made her feel good. Tonight wasn't for exploring that, though. No, tonight was about making her mine. About her making me hers.

Using my legs, I spread her thighs wide until her opening was right over my dick. Still holding on to her ass, I rubbed her up and down the length. Hell. I gritted my teeth as her wet heat felt so good that my balls tightened. She moaned my name, her pussy flooding with more arousal to help me slip into her. When I felt her thighs begin to tremble, I took her hand and guided it down to my cock. Wrapping her fingers around the base, it took me a few moments before I could speak. "Put me inside you, *vita mia*. Make me a part of you."

Her eyes shot to mine, capturing my gaze and holding it hostage as she did just that. When the heat of her entrance brushed over the tip of my dick, I nearly lost what little control I had left. Nearly tossed her on her back and took what she was so selflessly giving me. I had to release her ass, although it nearly killed me to let her go. If I didn't stop touching her, I was going to hurt her.

Inch by inch she slid down my length. Her channel was soaking wet, her muscles soft and welcoming from her earlier release, but already starting to clench again, desperate for more. When the head of my dick hit with resistance, she clenched up, not pulling away from the pain that little wall of resistance promised, but not moving, either.

Fuck. I was about to explode and I was only halfway in her. She had to do this herself, though. I wouldn't take this from her. She had to give it to me. Her eyes filled with uncertainty. "Ciro…"

"I love you," I told her, forgetting about how close to the edge I was. Forgetting how good her heat felt surrounding my cock. Forgetting everything but the most important truth. "I love you more than anything. You are my life. Give this to me and I'll give you the world."

Tears filled her brown eyes, but in the next moment she was pushing her sweet heat down, and I was roaring with the feel of being seated to the hilt inside of paradise. She was panting, her entire body shaking with reaction. A tear fell onto my chest and my heart clenched at the sight of her crying.

"I'm sorry," I whispered. "I'm so sorry, *vita mia*."

She shook her head, a smile brightening the entire room. "Don't ever be sorry for this, Ciro. It's everything I've ever wanted." Slowly her body began to relax around my cock. She lowered her head and brushed her lips over my chin, my cheek, then my lips.

With that soft kiss I lost what small shred of control I had left. My hands reached for her ass, squeezing each globe in my hands hard. She moaned, her channel flooding with a wave of need as she quickly forgot about the pain. I thrust upward, felt her inner muscles quiver.

Cursing, I rolled us until she was underneath me. Her legs wrapped around my waist. I'd had fantasies about those damn legs. How they would bend around me and hold me prisoner while I fucked us both into next week. That was another thing for a different day.

Nothing about this moment would ever be categorized as fucking. Tonight, I made love to her. Maybe it was a little rougher than I had hoped, but it was hard to hold back when I finally had the only thing I'd ever truly wanted beneath me. As I felt my release building, she dropped over the edge, pulling me with her as her sweet, hot pussy milked me of every drop of come I'd been saving just for her.

Chapter 22

Scarlett

I knew I wasn't in my own bed, but this morning I didn't mind. The beast of a man I was wrapped around was the best pillow I'd ever had. The silky soft covers over us weren't needed because his heat was enough to melt through the polar icecaps. I snuggled against his chest, in that blissful in-between stage of asleep and awake.

My entire body was languid and sore in the most delicious way. Thinking about all the things Ciro had done to me to make my body ache made me squirm against him and need began to burn low in my belly. The big man shifted beside me, pressed his lips to the top of my head and fell straight back to sleep. Apparently I'd worn him out just as thoroughly as he had me.

His cellphone going off a few minutes later made us both groan. I cracked open an eye, saw that it was after ten in the morning and reached for a pillow to throw at the bedside table in hopes of shutting the damn phone up. Ciro reached blindly for it and I swatted at his hand. "No."

"It might be important, *vita mia*," he murmured, before brushing his lips over mine.

"Please?" I pouted. "Can't we have just a few more hours?"

His deep chuckle vibrated through my entire body, turning my burn into an inferno. "You have me for the rest of your life, baby. Let me get this."

I wasn't happy about it, but I didn't argue any more. Turning on my side away from him, I pulled a pillow over my head to block out the sun trying to peek through the window. I heard Ciro growl at the caller even as he molded his big body to mine, pressing his hard chest against my back.

"Ma." His growl disappeared. "Yeah, Ma. She's right here beside me…When? Think you can get everything planned in two weeks?"

I heard his mother scream, then start yelling at him, and my pout completely disappeared. I grinned and tossed the pillow aside, loving that he was being chastised by his mother. Obviously he'd told her he was planning to ask me to marry him and she had been impatiently waiting to find out what I had said.

I turned my head to watch Ciro's face. His eyes were glued to the sight of my ass, however, and he wasn't even paying attention to what Mary was yelling in his ear. I tapped him on the cheek, forcing his blue eyes up to mine as my pussy grew wet with want. He dropped the phone and cupped my jaw as he lowered his head to devour my mouth.

The kiss went on for an eternity, but ended far too soon. I was panting, ready to climb on top of him and have another taste of the ecstasy he could give me. But Mary was yelling even louder now and I could hear her just as plainly as if she were standing beside us.

"I can't plan a fucking wedding in two weeks." I was pretty sure I'd never heard Mary utter a curse word in my entire life, but her son asking her to plan our wedding in so short a time had shot her over the edge. "Ciro Donati, don't even think about doing that to me. That girl needs a dress. And there are flowers and a cake to arrange. How the hell am I going to get all of that done?"

I couldn't contain the happy giggle that bubbled up. Ciro dropped his head, burying his face in the valley between my breasts as he tried to hide his own laughter. Taking pity on the woman who was about to become my mother-in-law, I grabbed the phone and lifted it to my ear. "Mary?" Her yelling was effectively cut off and I heard her blow out a frustrated breath.

"I'm so happy you said yes to my idiot son, but seriously, Scarlett, I can't put together a wedding in that short a time frame."

My fingers stroked over Ciro's head and his entire body seemed to melt against mine. His weight pressed me into the mattress, his hand moving to stroke over my leg. I could have lain like that for the rest of my life. This was paradise to me.

"Mary, I don't need a big wedding. All I need is your son and a priest. Everything else is irrelevant," I tried to explain.

"Maybe to you," she burst out. "But this will be my son's only wedding. It will be big and it will be beautiful and you will both suck it up and deal with it. Now, do you think your grandmother and cousin Allegra will be able to come over from Sicily and help me? And Victoria. She will definitely have to come home. You can't get married without her as your maid of honor."

I pulled the phone away from my mouth as she continued to make plans that apparently didn't include either me or her son. Ciro lifted his head until he met my gaze. "She's lost her mind," I whispered.

"Let her have her fun, *vita mia*. All that matters to me is that you show up at the church ready to marry me." He reached for my left hand, pressed his lips to my ring finger and then dropped his head back onto my chest.

It was only then that I actually looked at the ring he'd put on my finger the night before. What the holy hell? That wasn't a ring. It was a little bit of platinum with a huge-ass rock on it. It needed its own zip code it was so big. I didn't understand how my hand didn't feel like it weighed twenty pounds, because that diamond sure as hell must have weighed that much. As I brought it closer, the little bit of sunlight streaming through the window hit the diamond, nearly blinding me.

"Where did you get this ring?" I was doing a little yelling of my own now.

He snorted. "I knew you didn't look at it. Fuck, Scarlett. You're the only woman I know who doesn't care what a guy puts on her finger. If I didn't love you so damn much I would be hurt."

"Oh, fuck you." I pushed him off me, sat up and looked at the ring better, completely forgetting that Mary was still on the phone. He knew I wasn't into material things. I didn't need expensive things. Or huge diamonds that looked like it was straight out of some blood diamond mine. "Tell me where you got the ring, Ciro."

Grunting, he pushed himself up onto his elbow. Those blue eyes were laughing at me as he grasped my left wrist and waved my hand back and forth, making the light sparkle off the diamond again. "This was something my great grandmother cherished. My great grandfather was a diamond merchant and when this came into his possession the old woman claimed it as her own. She wouldn't let anyone touch it, least of all her husband who wanted to cut it up to make several engagement rings. When she died, she left it to my father, and made him promise not to give it to me until he was sure I had found someone I planned on spending eternity with."

My heart skipped a beat as I listened to him speak. He was playing with my fingers as he did so, and I wasn't sure if he even realized he was doing it. His blue eyes were bright with a mixture of amusement, found memories of a woman he had only met a few times before she'd passed away, and love. So much love. For me.

"I told my father I was going to marry you and he gave me the diamond. Ma wanted me to have it cut into something smaller because she knows how you are, but even though I love you more than life, I couldn't bring myself to do that to something the old lady loved so much." He shrugged. "Like you, she meant a lot to me. With that ring on your finger, I feel like I'm cherishing her memory."

Suddenly, the ring—even as ostentatiously huge as it was—felt like the most precious thing that had ever belonged to me. I threw my arms around his neck, knocking him back onto the bed. "I love it," I told him. "I love it and I love you."

His arms wrapped around my shoulder, his fingers tangling in my hair.

"Scarlett? Scarlett? Are you still there? Ciro? Damn it," I vaguely heard Mary yelling through the phone. "I'm calling your grandmother, Scarlett," she yelled before hanging up.

She could call anyone she wanted. I had other things to do.

Like show Ciro Donati how much I loved the ring he'd put on my finger. I wasn't nervous like I had been the night before. He'd shown me he liked everything I did to him. Everything. My fingers were already tracing over his abs. I reached the head of his already straining cock before I'd even gotten to his belly button. The tip was already coated in his pre-cum. As I wrapped my hand around his girth, he released a hissing breath through his teeth.

"You keep that up and you won't be able to walk for a few days, *vita mia*."

I turned my head so my chin was over his heart and I could see his face. His eyes were dark and hungry. I shifted my hips until my drenched pussy lips were rubbing against the base of his cock, teasing us both. My mouth fell open, a soft whimper escaping.

"I'm willing to take that chance," I assured him as I pushed myself up until I was straddling his waist. I tilted my hips, enjoying the feel of his length pressed against my clit.

His rough hands cupped my ass, squeezing it in a way that exhilarated me. I felt his index fingers trace over the seam of my ass and shivered. How would that feel? Would I like it as much as that little caress promised I would?

Ciro was watching me closely, a ghost of a smile on his lips as he squeezed each cheek harder. "Not today, *vita mia*. You aren't ready for that yet."

I bit down on my lip but nodded, trusting him to ease me into the things I was so curious about. I wrapped my hand around his cock and he lifted me until it was positioned at my entrance. With our eyes still locked on each other, I slowly slid down.

My inner muscles were sore, but I loved how his hardness stretched the tender flesh. I took every inch slowly, not stopping until I was seated fully on him once more. His hands eased their hold on my ass until he was rubbing over the globes, encouraging me to go at my own pace.

"I'm yours, Scarlett." I nodded. "Say it. Tell me I'm yours."

I swallowed the sudden lump that filled my throat. It was too much, having him inside of me like this, knowing he loved me. Yet it wasn't nearly enough. "You're mine," I whispered.

He sat up, still deep inside of me. My arms wrapped around his neck, holding on as his hips thrust upward, blinding me for a few moments with how good it felt. My head fell onto his shoulder, my hair falling around us.

"Always," his raspy voice growled in my ear.

"Always," I echoed.

Ciro

I couldn't bring myself to let Scarlett out of my bed until almost dinnertime and only then because she started complaining she was hungry. My own stomach was growling loudly, reminding me that we hadn't eaten since dinner the night before.

With her giggling in my ear, she stuffed her arms into one of my shirts and I carried her into my kitchen. I hadn't been home much lately. Hell, I couldn't honestly remember when the last time I had been in my own apartment was. Luckily I had a housekeeper come in every few days to keep the place clean and the fridge stocked.

Reluctantly I set her on the island in the middle of the kitchen. Pressing a kiss to her forehead, I opened the fridge behind me and started pulling out ham, salami and prosciutto. Handing them all to her, I grabbed the bag of freshly washed lettuce and a tomato. My stomach growled louder as I took out the cheese and turned around.

Catching Scarlett checking out my naked ass had my dick hardening yet again. After spending nearly twenty-four hours in bed with this woman, I was still insatiable. Seeing how my body responded to just her eyes touching me, pink filled her cheeks and her mouth fell open in a soft little gasp.

"Don't even think about it," I cautioned as I set everything on the island beside her. "You need to recover a little first."

Her bottom lip pouted out at me. "But I want you again."

My dick flexed at the sound of her husky voice saying those words. Fuck, I ached for her so badly it was like we hadn't just spent an entire day exploring each other's bodies. But she was already raw from our lovemaking and I didn't want to cause her more pain. We needed a distraction, because I knew if we stayed home that night we'd be in bed for another full day.

I gave her a quick kiss, not trusting myself to linger. "First, I'm going to feed you. Then we're going to shower—in separate bathrooms so I don't make love to you against the damn wall—and then we're going out."

"Out?" She frowned as she watched me put together our sandwiches. "Out where?"

I shrugged. "We could go to a club, since I know how much you enjoy those." I smirked when she rolled her eyes at me. "Or a movie."

"Pass," she grumbled and stole a slice of ham from the container I was holding.

"We could go back to the compound and spend the evening with your father." Vito had tried calling me a few times throughout the day, but Scarlett had threatened bodily harm if I dared touch my phone again. I wasn't scared of what she would do to me, but I'd wanted to make her happy so I'd let him and anyone else who dared call go straight to voicemail.

"We can see Papa tomorrow." I finished putting the sandwiches together and offered her one. Her eyes brightened at the sight of it. "You've never made me food before."

"Lie." I kissed the tip of her nose. "I made you popcorn when you were fifteen."

Her sexy laugh was like a shot of pure lust straight to my dick. I kept my stomach pressed against the island so she couldn't see how hard I was getting just standing there laughing and eating with her. "That doesn't count. You put a bag in the microwave. This is different."

She was right. This was different. I hadn't loved her then like I loved her now. Making the woman I loved more than life something to eat was a hell of a lot different than making a snack for a girl I'd considered family.

We ate in silence for a few minutes before she spoke again. "I don't want to go out. Can't we stay here if I promise not to do naughty things to you?"

"I don't trust myself not to keep my hands off you, baby." I pulled bottles of water from the fridge for us. "Besides, I want to show you off a little. Let the world know that you're mine."

"I could tattoo 'Ciro's Woman' across my forehead and no one would ever question it again," she offered with a grin.

The thought of my name tattooed on her only made my dick ache more. I took our plates and tossed them in the sink, not caring if I broke them or not. Turning back to her, I grabbed her around the waist and tossed her over my shoulder.

Scarlett screamed, then started laughing. “Where are we going?”

“You’re going to take a long, hot bath and I’m going to take a fucking ice-cold shower. Then, we’re going to go out, because I’m about to fuck you until neither one of us can stand up straight.” I smacked her on the ass but quickly rubbed the slight sting away.

“But I don’t want to go out,” she whined.

“I’ll buy you coffee,” I bribed.

“It’d better be really good coffee,” she muttered as I entered the bedroom and headed for the connecting bathroom.

Chapter 23

Scarlett

Mary had been busy while I'd been locked away in Ciro's apartment the day before. By the time we got back to the compound the next day, it was to find that we had an entire house full of guests. My uncle Gio met us at the door and, after giving me a kiss on the cheek, he pulled Ciro toward my father's office.

I didn't know how Mary had gotten my Nona to get on a plane and actually set foot in the States, but there she was sitting in the living room with my cousin Allegra. I loved my grandmother. She was the kind of old-school Italian woman who wasn't happy unless she was cooking for her family. She didn't take anything off anyone, least of all her firstborn—my father. She didn't care if he was the head of the *Cosa Nostra* or not. When she told him to do something, he jumped to get it done. During the three years Victoria and I had lived with her at the Sicilian compound where she lived with Allegra and my uncle, we'd really gotten to know each other better.

As I walked into the living room, Allegra jumped to her feet and I hurried forward to hug her. Allegra might have grown up in Sicily under the ever watchful eye of her father and Nona, but she'd spent her holidays with me and Victoria in New York. The three of us had always been close and I was happy to see her because if I was going to have a huge wedding like Mary was determined to put together, I wanted her there as one of my bridesmaids.

My cousin and I didn't look anything alike. Where I was tall she was small. Her jet-black hair was long and glossy, her eyes exotically tilted like a feline and as dark as a moonless night. Allegra was voluptuous and I had been jealous of all her curves since she'd started getting breasts. She was a few months older than I was, but she had been so sheltered by her parents that she seemed younger.

"It feels like I haven't seen you in months rather than just a few weeks," Allegra said with a laugh as we pulled apart. "I've missed you and Victoria."

"I'm so glad you're here." I hugged her again. "It hasn't been the same without you around."

"Well, let's look at this ring."

I released Allegra at Nona's commanding tone and offered her my hand before I even realized I was doing it. The old woman's eyes widened when she saw how big the uncut diamond was, but she didn't question Ciro's choice to give me something she knew I would normally scoff at. For about two minutes I'd hated the ring. When he'd told me it had belonged to his great grandmother and how much it had meant to her, I'd fallen in love with it hard.

"Oh, my goodness," Allegra murmured as she stood with Nona to look at the ring. "It's beautiful, Scarlett. I'd be so scared I'd lose it if I were you."

"The boy did good," Nona finally said with approval in her thickly accented English. "The two of you will have a good, strong marriage."

I already knew that, but it was nice to have her approval. Victoria could do no wrong in Nona's eyes, but she had always been a little tough on me. That she was giving Ciro her stamp of approval only added to my happiness right then. "Thank you, Nona."

"Scarlett?"

I turned at the sound of my twin's voice to find her already running into the room. Her face was pale. She looked tired, but there was a smile on her face. "Mary called me yesterday and told me to get my butt home. Something about you agreeing to marry her thick-headed son."

Seeing the strain on her face dimmed some of my own pleasure at seeing her. I'd spoken to her almost every day over the last week and I'd known she had things on her mind, but I hadn't even imagined that it was taking this kind of a toll on her. She looked as if she'd lost weight and from the shadows under her eyes I knew she wasn't sleeping.

"Tor…" I saw her sway as she neared, watched as what little color she still had in her cheeks vanished. I reached for her as did Allegra and Nona, but she was already falling.

I got to her just as her head hit the floor and I dropped to my knees beside her. Nona cried out loudly enough to bring the guards running, but I paid them no attention as they filled the room. I knew what was wrong, knew she probably hadn't been keeping as close an eye on her blood sugar levels as she should have. This was why I hated being away from her. This was why I worried about her so damn much.

"Get my son," Nona commanded in a shaky voice. "Hurry."

"I need to check her levels," I told Allegra. "Papa keeps a kit in the drawer of the coffee table."

She hurried over to the table and found the kit and was back within a few seconds. I would never get used to this happening. It scared the living hell out of me. As I prepped her finger so I could check her blood sugar levels, my hands shook. It took ten more seconds for the tester to give me the information I needed once I got a drop of Victoria's blood on the little strip.

Too high. Too high. Way too fucking high. There was a bottle of insulin and a syringe already in the kit, because Papa had always been worried about emergencies like this from the day we'd found out Victoria was a diabetic. She should have had an insulin pump, but Victoria had never liked dealing with them. Too stubborn. Too hardheaded. Too maddening. I wanted to wring her little neck, but I would miss her too much if I killed her. I filled the syringe with the insulin and then stabbed it into her thigh.

My heart was beating so fast and hard that I felt like I was going to throw up. I wanted to strangle my sister for letting her health go while she struggled with her feelings for a man who didn't deserve her. I wanted to stab Cristiano and Dante and even Anya who had been with her over the last week and obviously hadn't been taking care of her like they should have been.

We waited for nearly a minute, barely breathing as we waited to see if the insulin would help. I checked her pulse. It was weak, but slowly starting to grow stronger. I was ready to call for an ambulance when Victoria moaned and lifted fingers that shook to her head. "Scarlett?" she whispered.

"*Grazie a Dio*," Nona cried as she fell onto the couch. "That girl will be the death of me one day."

Allegra crouched down on the other side of her. "Don't try to move. Just let yourself recover for a little longer."

Tears filled her eyes. "Damn it. I should've known this was going to happen."

I couldn't speak. I was too upset. Too scared. Too pissed. I wanted to shake some sense into her, yell at her for putting herself at risk like she was doing. I wanted to cry because when she passed out like she just had I was terrified I would lose her. That she wouldn't ever wake up again. I wanted to scream and throw things and punch the people who had promised me they would watch out for my twin.

Papa ran into the room with Gio, Ciro and Cristiano. "Should we call an ambulance? Does she need to go to the hospital?" Nothing scared my father more than when Victoria had one of these episodes. His face was gray and there was sweat beaded on his forehead.

I was surprised to see Dante when he followed the other men into the living room. He hadn't come back to New York since Papa had sent him to Chicago over three years before. His darkly handsome face didn't show an ounce of emotion as his dark eyes took in everything happing around the room all at once.

I didn't spare him a second glance as I jumped to my feet and punched my brother in the face. His head snapped back because I'd caught him off guard. I was so mad I barely felt the pain that had shot through my fist and all the way up my arm to my shoulder.

Ciro caught me around the waist, pulling me away from his friend before I could hit him again. He didn't have to worry; I was done hitting him. Physical pain didn't do anything to Cristiano. He was a total freak when it came to pain. It was words that cut him deeper than anything else. "What the hell have you been doing? Huh? Do you know how high her blood sugar was, Cristiano? Do you? It was over five hundred," I screamed at him. "Do you not care that she could die? Is your head so far up your own ass that you can't take five minutes to make sure our sister is okay?"

My brother rubbed at his jaw, but the look on his face suggested he was just as upset as I was. There was no way he could be that upset. No way he could understand that the mere thought of losing my twin was my worst nightmare. "She checked it when she got on the plane this morning, Scarlett. She was fine. I swear to you I've been making sure that she checks her blood sugar levels."

"Scarlett," Victoria's weak voice called to me.

I pulled away from Ciro and went back to kneel beside her. Her fingers were cold and still trembling but her coloring was slowly coming back. I felt her pulse, relieved when it felt stronger than it had only a few minutes before.

"Don't be mad at anyone, Scarlett," she pleaded. "I was fine this morning. I started feeling bad on the ride from the airport and I should've checked my sugar then."

"Yes, you fucking should have," I scolded as I lost the hold on my tears and let them fall. "Stop doing this shit to me, Tor."

Her smile was weak but I saw a spark of her normally happy self in there. "Sorry. I'll do better." She turned her head, looking up at our father, who was slowly calming down. "Tell them to let me up, Papa. I'm fine now."

"Maybe you should see the doctor, Victoria," Allegra suggested in her soft voice.

"I'm fine, really."

I scrubbed a hand over my face, wiping away my tears. "You can get up, but you're going to bed."

Her eyes narrowed on me. "I can't go to bed. Mary has plans for us. We have to find you a dress, and Allegra and I need one too. I swear to you, I'm fine. Damn it, Scarlett. Don't baby me now when we have so much to do."

Everyone was going to drive me crazy over this damn wedding. I shot Ciro a glance, saw that he was watching me closely, and shook my head at him. "There has to be an easier way. Can't you just kidnap your mother and tie her up until we're married?"

His chuckle helped ease some of the tension that was making every muscle in my body ache. "I have a better idea."

"A better idea than eloping?" I muttered.

"Definitely." He offered me his hand and helped me to my feet. "Come on. You'll like it."

Papa helped Victoria to her feet, but his arm stayed around her waist as he guided her over to the couch where she sat down beside Nona. Whatever Ciro's plan was, it had better not involve us having to leave the house. My sister needed to rest and I was too nervous to leave her. Screw a dress.

Three hours later we were still in the living room. Mary had joined us and for some reason so had Anya. The guys had disappeared back into my father's office when Benito had arrived with Mary. I figured they were all hiding from the woman since she had brought an entire book of things for us to talk about before the wedding could take place, in her eyes.

In one corner of the room, one of New York's most sought-after wedding dress designers was setting up shop with sample dresses that two models were supposed to show us. They were already showing off two different designs for bridesmaid dresses. If I hadn't loved Ciro before, I would have fallen for him when he'd made a few phone calls and had the designer and her models delivered to the front door. He was doing everything he possibly could to make this easier on me and I could never show him how much his thoughtfulness meant to me.

In the kitchen two caterers had set up sample platters for us to try. One was doing the actual food while the other was going to make the cake. A florist did a Skype chat with us, showing off different bouquet ideas that Mary had emailed her about the night before.

Victoria was looking better. She wasn't nearly as pale as she had been. She was even eating a few of the sample *hor d'oeuvres*. I wouldn't have asked her to come home myself, not when I'd known she was trying to sort out everything concerning Adrian in her head, but I was glad she was there nonetheless. It would have felt wrong to have a big wedding without my twin—the other half of myself—there to share the day with me.

It was nearly five hours after the designer had arrived before we were actually done. I'd picked out my dress with the help of all the women in my life, picked out what we were going to eat at the reception and even gotten Ciro out of Papa's office to help me decide what flavor the cake should be. The bouquets were already being made and the measurements taken so an entire team of seamstresses could work on altering the dresses.

Everything had been sorted in less than a day and I hadn't even had to leave the house. Ciro had pulled off a small miracle and I wondered if maybe he'd wanted a big wedding all along. The way he had made everything available so readily told me that our wedding was more important to him than he had originally let me think.

Chapter 24

Ciro

"So you're telling me that Jr is back in my city?"

I tossed back the last of my coffee, trying to get the taste of cake out of my mouth. I'd tasted six different cake samples to make Scarlett happy and one of them had been butterscotch. That little minx knew I hated the taste of butterscotch, but her giggles as I'd put that damn little square of cake in my mouth was worth the bad taste that still lingered on my tongue.

While the women were busy sorting out wedding plans, I'd been in Vito's office catching up on all the shit I'd missed the day before. A day didn't mean anything to some people, but for me it was the difference between five things needing my attention and two hundred.

Dante De Stefano scratched at his beard, his eyes hooded as always. I'd known the man just as long as I had Cristiano. The three of us had been friends all our lives, but Dante kept a part of himself guarded even more than I did. "He left Chicago about two days ago, but I didn't know until last night. Senior sent him back when he found out about Fontana disappearing."

"We all know that Fontana was the brains behind Jr's businesses." Vito lifted his glass of scotch and took a large swallow. "With him out of the picture, what little ground Jr has gained here will quickly fall apart. That means he will send someone else to take over for him and try to keep Jr in line. My gut tells me it will be Fontana's brother."

"If that's the case then we need to keep our eyes open. Enzo is a sick sonofabitch," Cristiano muttered, touching his fingers gingerly to his bruised cheek where Scarlett had hit him earlier.

He didn't have to tell any of us that. Enzo was worse than Jr with how much fun he liked to have with unwilling women—hell, unwilling anything. And he would be after answers to who had been behind his brother's disappearance. Ultimately, that was my doing but I wasn't worried about Enzo. I could handle that prick if he wanted to dish out a little revenge for his brother.

It was Scarlett I worried about. It was one of the major reasons I'd been so hesitant to get involved with her in the first place. My job required me to do certain things for the good of the *Cosa Nostra*, and that put a target not only on my back, but on anyone who was close to me.

She would be safer if I'd never told her I loved her. No one would touch her if she didn't become my wife. I should just tell her that everything was off, send her back to Sicily with her grandmother and Gio and pretend I'd never met her.

Just thinking those things made my heart stop. I was a selfish bastard because now that I'd had a taste of what it felt like when Scarlett told me she loved me, how she fell apart in my arms when I was deep inside her, waking up to her beside me in bed—I couldn't let her go. I would make sure she was protected, even if that meant locking her in our apartment and never letting her out of the house without me.

Fuck, she would kick my ass for even trying to send her away at this point. And I would let her.

"We'll worry about Enzo later. First, I want Jr found. Take care of him once and for all." Vito shot me a dirty look, letting me know loud and clear he thought I was the reason why Scarlett had turned down his offer of dealing with Jr herself. I didn't care why she'd done it; I was just thankful she had. "Dante, I want you to stick around and help these boys out. I want the bastard taken out before the wedding."

"I'll be sticking around for a little while. I wouldn't miss Scarlett's wedding for anything, and you know that I want Jr's head just as much as anyone else here." Dante sat forward in his chair, his hooded eyes darkening even more than normal. "But when I leave, I don't want to go back to Chicago alone."

Every eye but mine turned on him in curiosity. Mine were on Vito, who looked almost gleeful, as if he suspected what his underboss was talking about. "And who would you be taking with you?" Vito's voice didn't betray his pleasure at what he thought the man was going to say next.

"Allegra."

Gio shot to his feet, cursing in rapid-fire Italian so furiously there was spittle flying out of his mouth. Vito's eyes darkened. I was sure he—like the others in the room—where expecting him to say Victoria. It had always been something Vito had been vocal about. Wanting Dante to marry one of his daughters.

I'd already suspected it would be Allegra, though. Scarlett had told me some interesting things about Dante the day before. Things I never would have suspected of the man I'd grown up with. She knew him a lot better than I obviously did, and if I hadn't known she was mine, I might have been jealous of how close she was with him.

Fuck. There was no might about it. I was jealous despite knowing she was mine. No man wanted his woman to be close to any man who wasn't related to her by blood. Especially when that man looked like Dante.

"She's going home with me," Gio said, finally calmed down enough to speak English, but his accent was thick and almost unintelligible. "You will not get your hands on my daughter, De Stefano. I will not allow it."

I hadn't needed Scarlett to tell me that her uncle was not a fan of Dante's. I'd always known it. Even when we were kids, I'd felt the animosity Vito's brother held for Dante and his father. I'd never asked why and I'd never cared enough to find out. Scarlett probably knew, though, and now that I was seeing the animosity pouring off of Gio, my curiosity was piqued.

Dante didn't betray his emotions by so much as a flick of his lashes. Even in the face of Gio's rage he was completely calm. Keeping his eyes on Vito, he spoke with an almost detachedness. "You asked me something a few days ago, Vito. I told you I couldn't because it wouldn't be fair to either Victoria or myself. She's like a sister to me and marrying her would be wrong. I want Allegra. She's your niece, your blood. If she were mine, you would have your connection. Isn't that what you wanted all along?"

Gio started raging again in Italian, throwing his hands in the air and calling the younger man names that, had it been me he was yelling at, I would have already knocked his teeth down his throat. Dante didn't defend himself, but I saw him turn to cold stone before my eyes as he continued to look at nothing but Vito.

Vito let his brother continue to yell for several minutes, his eyes blank as he thought over what Dante had just said. When he spoke, however, it wasn't to Dante but to my father. "How would you handle this, Ben?"

My father shifted in his chair, shooting Gio a disapproving glare before turning to his best friend. "I would want to know how Allegra felt. This isn't the Dark Ages, Vito. Handing the girl over into a relationship she might not want is a little barbaric, if you ask me."

He nodded. "I agree."

Gio turned wild eyes on his brother, a snarl twisting his lips. I hadn't noticed until then that the two men didn't look much alike. I could see Scarlett's grandmother in the older brother, but Gio must have looked like their father. "What do you agree with? What the hell could you possibly agree to where this piece of shit and my daughter are concerned?"

Vito held up a hand, calm in the face of Gio's rage and effortlessly stopping the younger Vitucci in his tracks. "Allegra should be given the chance to decide for herself if she wants to be with Dante. If she accepts him, then I'll let her go with him when he decides to return to Chicago."

"The fuck you will. This is my daughter you're just handing over to him. Mine, not yours. You don't have the right to allow *my* child to do shit."

Vito's eyes lost the blank look and a cold anger settled over his features. "Let go of the past, *fratello*. Let it go before it destroys you. Allegra is a grown woman, not a child any longer. Remember that, Gio. She can make her own choices and if she chooses Dante, I will agree to the marriage. It will make us stronger. Even you cannot deny that."

There was a sharp tap on the door, forcing the two brothers to shut up. Gio marched over to the window, staring out at the scenery. His shoulders were stiff, anger rolling off him in waves. Cristiano stood and moved to open the door, showing us that Scarlett stood on the other side. My heart kicked painfully in my chest, and I ached to pull her onto my lap and just hold her. The look on her face told me she'd heard at least a little of what her father had said, but she didn't mention it as she stepped inside.

"Whatever business you're all talking in here, I think it can be concluded. You've spent hours in this stuffy old office." She moved across the room and stopped behind Dante's chair. She put her hands on his shoulders, effortlessly letting us all know that she was on his side regardless of why the two older Vituccis were yelling over him. I had the strongest urge to shoot the other man in the back of the head. Even though she was mine, even though she was wearing my ring, I couldn't stand the thought of her touching someone else even as innocently as she was.

Then her eyes fell on me and I saw the blaze of love and need in her brown eyes, and my jealousy turned to ashes instantly.

"I'm ready to go home, Ciro." The way she said my name had every fine hair on my body standing at attention along with my dick. Her voice was a caress that soothed every tense muscle and brought my heart back to life after spending so many hours talking business.

Home, she said. I'd never really thought of my apartment as that before, but now it was exactly how I saw it. Because of her. I jumped to my feet, itching to throw her over my shoulder like a damn caveman and carry her back to my apartment—our home.

"You are home," Vito said as he stood, nearly as upset as his brother now. "Just because you're marrying this boy doesn't mean you are moving out of your home. I won't allow it. You're safer here, *passerotta*."

Gio grumbled something under his breath about the shoe on the other foot, but no one paid him any attention.

Scarlett shook her head. "No, Papa. This is your home. Mine is with Ciro now. And I'm just as safe if not more so at the apartment." She walked around the desk and kissed his cheek, softening the blow of her words a little. "I'll see you tomorrow."

He blew out a long, tired breath. "Okay, *passerotta*." He gave me a hard glare. "Watch over her or I'll kill you." It wasn't an idle threat. He was completely serious. I would have been stupid not to believe he meant it.

I merely nodded. There weren't enough words in any language that I could use to promise him I would watch over her until the last breath left my body. He already knew it anyway.

Scarlett came back to me, holding out her left hand. My great grandmother's diamond seemed to wink up at me before my own hand swallowed hers. I pulled her against me, brushing my lips over hers without caring that everyone was watching.

"Let's go home, *vita mia*."

Chapter 25

Scarlett

Everything was set. Mary was taking care of all the small details that still had to be wrapped up before the wedding, so all I had to do was sit back and relax.

Or stay in bed with Ciro all day.

He was indulging my need to have him stay in bed with me for most of the day even though he should have been working. With Dante still in New York, he was taking advantage and letting me keep him in our bed until late afternoon. If I knew I could have this every day for the rest of my life, I would beg my father to make Dante stay and pick someone else to deal with business in Chicago.

There were only two more days until the wedding, and I was supposed to meet everyone at the dress designer's studio so we could all do the last fitting, but I was taking my time. Ciro was making it hard not to blow it all off and stay in for the rest of the day. Fuck the dress and anyone else. I was about to explode for him, damn it. That was ten times more important.

His lips pressed into the valley between my breasts as his fingers teased at my pussy lips, making me tilt my hips upward in a silent plea. I felt his cock flex against my outer thigh, his pre-cum marking my skin, silently telling me that he was just as far gone as I was and we hadn't even gotten started yet.

I spread my thighs wider, opening for him. His breath hissed out through his teeth as he dipped two fingers into my opening and felt how wet I was for him. "Already?"

I licked my dry lips, panting hard as he fingered me. "Always."

Ciro growled and moved so fast my head felt like it was going to spin off as he got to his knees and flipped me onto my stomach like I weighed nothing at all. His calloused hands gripped my hips, lifting them until I was at the perfect angle to take him. He positioned the head of his cock at my entrance, but didn't do more than push the head inside.

He bent, pressing his lips to the small of my back, making my heart clench with love. Lower, my pussy was doing some clenching too. Ciro groaned and thrust his hips forward roughly. I cried out at the delicious invasion. I loved it when he couldn't control himself. Loved that I was the one making him lose it.

One arm wrapped around my waist, trapping me against him. The other lifted higher, squeezing and massaging one breast and then the other as he pulled back and thrust deep and hard once again. My head fell to the mattress as that quickly I lost all thought except for how good this man felt inside my body.

All too soon my release was rushing up on me and I tried to pull away, not wanting to come yet. Ciro wouldn't let me, though. His hands gripped either side of my waist, his fingers biting into my flesh as he thrust harder, faster. I cried out as his cock hit a spot that felt so good I forgot how to breathe for a few seconds.

With a curse, Ciro released one hand on my waist and grabbed my hair, wrapping it around his wrist so he could pull my head back until he could kiss me. His tongue thrust into my mouth just as roughly as his cock was my pussy. His sweaty chest rubbed against my back, helping our bodies slide against each other as he changed the angle.

"Fuck, Scarlett. I can't get enough," he rasped at my ear.

There wasn't enough air in my lungs to tell him it was the same for me. I'd never be able to get enough of him, of this.

The hand still on my waist tightened and he shifted, falling onto his back and taking me with him while still keeping our bodies connected. My hair fell over his shoulder and his teeth sank into the tender flesh just under my ear, driving me mad with a need that would never burn out. He flattened his hand against my lower stomach, trapping me easily in place as he lifted our hips off the mattress and thrust into me from behind.

"Oh, God," I whispered as my release started to build. My thighs clenched, but he forced them to stay apart as my entire body tried to lock up with the force of the building orgasm. "Oh, God," I whimpered.

His hand moved lower, his thumb finding my clit and flicking over it twice before pressing down hard. The entire room exploded with a kaleidoscope of colors as I came apart for him. "Ciro," I cried, my head thrashing from side to side on his chest. "Oh, God, Ciro. Please."

"Say it, *vita mia.* Say the words you know I ache for."

Even in my mindlessness I knew what he wanted. He always wanted them when he was close to the edge of his own release. I gave them to him. "I love you," I screamed as he thrust faster, taking my pleasure to a whole new level. "I love you," I said again. "I'll love you forever."

"Fuck," he bellowed as I felt him thicken even more inside me and the first hot shot of his release filled me. He didn't stop until I'd taken every last drop and then his hips fell onto the mattress, his arms folding over my stomach as he gasped for breath. "I love you," he said against my ear before he kissed my neck.

I turned onto my stomach, still lying on top of him. I was exhausted, but my body felt like it was glowing. I laid my ear over his heart, counting the crazy-fast beats as it slowly found its way back to normal. We were both covered in sweat, but the AC was quickly chilling our overheated bodies.

Ciro stroked one hand down my back and over my ass, then back up again, his touch making every nerve in my body tingle even after the mind-blowing orgasm he'd just given me. We lay like that for a long while before I felt his entire body stiffen beneath me. Concerned, I lifted my head to look at him.

"What's wrong?"

He had that blank look on his face and my heart filled with lead. Why would he hide his emotions from me now?

"Are you on the pill?"

My brows lifted at that question. Had he just now remembered birth control? We'd made love at least a hundred times and he hadn't thought about it until now? "No, of course I'm not," I told him as I sat up. "There's never been a reason to take the pill or any other birth control."

And I hadn't worried about it once over the last fifteen days. He hadn't mentioned it and I thought he just wanted to start our family sooner rather than later. I wasn't against the idea so I hadn't questioned his not using anything to protect us. I wanted a family with him. I wanted his child growing inside me.

The look that crossed his face was there for only a second before it was gone, but I'd seen it. Had I ever seen Ciro Donati scared? No, not even the night I'd been hurt. He'd been shaken, yes, but if he'd been scared he'd hid it well.

He jumped out of bed in a single fluid move, leaving me sitting there with my heart filling heavy with dread. What was happening? "Ciro—"

"You're already late for your fitting appointment. You should get ready. My mother will be waiting," he called over his shoulder as he started for the bathroom.

A lump filled my throat at his dismissive tone, but anger started to boil in my veins. I was confused and hurt and I didn't understand anything that was going on right then. We'd gone from making love, to holding each other, to him turning into a complete stranger in only a matter of minutes. All because I wasn't on the pill?

"What's going on, Ciro?" I demanded as I jumped out of bed and followed him into the bathroom. "What just happened?"

He kept his back to me as he turned on the shower. "Nothing."

"Bullshit." I grasped his arm in both of mine and tugged him around to face me. His eyes were blank, his face set in neutral lines that didn't tell me anything he was thinking. That hurt more than anything. He was shutting me out. "If you don't want a baby right now, tell me. I can see the doctor." Even though I hated them, I would go and get put on the pill. We were still young; we didn't have to start our family immediately.

Unless I was already pregnant.

"I don't want a baby." His voice was cold, empty.

I nodded, still confused, but I nodded anyway. "Okay. So I'll get on the pill and we can talk about having a baby in a few years."

His eyes became more hooded. "I don't want a baby. Ever. I don't want kids, Scarlett."

I stepped back, feeling like he'd just slapped me. I'd never thought of not having kids. Maybe they hadn't been forefront in my thoughts, but I'd always wanted them. I'd always wanted to be a mother and when I'd pictured myself with a baby on my hip I'd always seen this man as its father. "Why?"

Ciro shrugged. "I have my reasons."

Anger was a hell of a lot better than hurt. As it built I used it to push aside the pain that was filling my chest. "That's not an answer, Ciro. Talk to me. I need to know why you don't want kids."

"Because I don't want to put an innocent little kid through having to face the fact that his father is a monster," he exploded, and for the first time I took a step back from him in the face of his anger. Not because I was scared of him. I would never be scared of this man. He wouldn't physically hurt me, ever.

I stepped back because he'd thrown me completely off center with that admission. He wasn't just angry, he was scared and hurting. Monster? I could see that it was exactly how he thought of himself. All my anger at him, all the hurt, evaporated as I began to understand why he was so set against becoming a father.

I moved until I was only a few inches from him and laid my palm flat against his chest, right over his heart. "A monster couldn't love me as much as you do, Ciro. You're a good man and I love you completely."

His big shoulders drooped. "No, Scarlett. I'm just really good at pretending. Underneath all of this, I'm not even human. I've done things that would haunt a normal person. There is other's blood on my hands and it's tainted me until there's nothing left but the part that loves you. I don't have anything left over for anyone else."

My heart was breaking for him, but I was at a loss for how to make him see he was wrong about himself. Lifting my hand, I cupped his jaw. He'd dropped the walls he'd put up and was letting me see all of himself now. There was true fear in his eyes. Fear that he couldn't love our child. That his baby might hate him. "I love you, and our child would love you too. I love you despite the things you might have done in the past." He opened his mouth, and I pressed my thumb to his lips. "Despite what you might have to do in the future. Doing those things doesn't make you a monster. Not in my eyes."

His arms wrapped around me and he lowered his head until his forehead pressed against mine. "*Vita mia…*"

"I'm not going to beg you and I know I can't convince you overnight, so I'm not going to argue with you about this. Not now, not ever." I stroked my fingers over his hair and he shuddered against me. He closed his eyes. "All I need in the world is your arms around me. Us having a baby would only add to how happy I am, but I understand that you can't wrap your mind around that right now."

"I might not ever be able to wrap my mind around it, Scarlett."

"Yes, I know." I sighed and pulled back until our eyes met, needing him to see how serious I was right then. "That's why I won't ever bring it up again. You are enough for me, Ciro. Nothing else will ever make me as happy as being loved by you. I'll go on the pill and we don't have to talk about this again for the rest of our lives. But if you ever change your mind, I'll be ready and waiting."

All the tension in him lifted and he lifted me in his arms. My legs wrapped around his waist and I met his hungry kiss. He was back to being the Ciro I loved wholeheartedly.

I didn't want to remind him that I could already be pregnant. Didn't want to think about what would happen if I was in fact already carrying his child. I only wanted to lose myself in his arms again.

Chapter 26

Scarlett

I was over two hours late for my appointment with the dress designer. Mary, Victoria, Nona, Allegra and Anya were already inside when I entered the studio with Paco and one of Ciro's other men at my side. My father had sent a few of his own men with Victoria, Nona and Allegra. Mary's usual guard was also taking up space at the door.

It looked like Paco was going to be my shadow whenever I went out without Ciro, but I was okay with that. I liked him just as much as I did Desi. It was the other guy who gave me the creeps. I wasn't a fan of Antony, and I never had been. Ciro wouldn't let me go anywhere without at least two of his men, though, so I had to put up with the man.

Victoria had asked me to make Anya a bridesmaid to even up the wedding party. I liked her and hadn't hesitated about agreeing with my sister. The little Russian was just finishing up her last fitting when I walked through the door. "You have got to be the only bride in the world who doesn't give a shit about her wedding."

I shrugged. "It's not about the wedding for me. It's about the man I'm marrying. All that matters is that he becomes my husband. As simples as that." I took a seat on the loveseat beside Allegra, who was sipping at champagne along with the other women.

Paco took up post behind me, but Antony stood right beside me, making me feel uncomfortable. Hell, he was kind of clingy. I moved closer to Allegra. "Paco, tell your man to stand by the door. He's breathing on me."

"Door," Paco commanded with a bite in his voice.

I didn't give the other man another thought once he moved away, but Anya watched him for a long moment before excusing herself to go change out of her dress.

Mary and Nona had been busy whispering back and forth to each other across the room and didn't even notice that I'd arrived until Mary turned around. "There you are," she said with a beaming smile. "Are you ready to try the dress on for the last time before you marry my son?"

A shot of excitement ran through me. Two more days and I was going to be Mrs. Ciro Donati. How could that not make my heart skip a beat and make me almost giggly with excitement?

"I can't wait," I told her honestly as I got to my feet.

Twenty minutes later, when the final pearl button was in place, I stepped in front of the mirrors in the front of the studio. With my veil on and my hair pulled back in a messy version of the hairstyle Victoria had been adamant that I have for the big day, I couldn't help gasping at the sight of my reflection. I'd never felt so beautiful in my life as I did right then.

Behind me, all the women had gone completely quiet and I turned to see what their reaction was. Nona had tears in her eyes, while Mary openly wept. Victoria and Allegra eyed me with appreciation and a little envy. It was Anya who was taking in everything with a critical eye, and finding nothing lacking.

"You're so beautiful," Mary told me as she stepped onto the small platform where the seamstress had told me to stand earlier so I could see the dress from every angle in the trio of mirrors. She hugged me carefully, trying not to mess up my dress in any way. "I can't believe you're going to be my daughter-in-law in just under forty-eight hours. It's more than I could ever ask for Ciro. I know the two of you will be happy together."

I tried to smile for her but wasn't sure I completely pulled it off. I wanted to make Ciro happy, wanted our life together. But despite telling myself not to worry about it, I couldn't keep my mind off the fact that I could possibly be pregnant right then.

Would he want me to get rid of it? Would he hate me because I couldn't? Would he stop loving me?

I pushed those thoughts away as soon as they entered my mind, and pretended that I didn't have a care in the world as Victoria and Allegra stood to gush over my dress and how good I looked in it. My sister didn't buy it for even a second, though, and when the seamstress took me back to the dressing room to help me change, Victoria came with me.

I tensed up, as the little woman undid the hundred pearl buttons, dreading this conversation with my sister. I felt her gaze on me grow more assessing with each tick of the clock on the wall. By the time the seamstress was done, my neck was beginning to ache with how much effort it was taking to keep from looking at my twin.

"I'll help her from here, Diane," Victoria told the woman, who gave her a bright smile and excused herself.

She stepped up behind me as she started pulling the dress open, her eyes trapping mine in the mirror. "Did you and Ciro have a fight?"

"No. We're fine." I let the dress fall to my waist, leaving me only in my strapless white bra. Reaching up, I pulled the clips from my hair and shook out the long red tresses.

"Then why do you look like you've had your heart ripped out and stomped on?"

I gave up trying to hide the truth from her. There was no use in trying anyway. Victoria was part of myself. Lying to her just wasn't possible. Not when she was in the same room with me anyway. "Ciro doesn't want kids."

"Oh." She bit her lip, obviously not expecting me to say that of all things. For several minutes she was quiet as she helped me undress. When I pulled my shoes back on she sat in one of the plush chairs in one of the corners of the dressing room. "Is that a deal breaker for you?"

"No," I told her honestly and sank into the other chair across from her. "I love him. Kids aren't a must for me, Tor. But…"

Her eyebrows lifted. "But?"

"I might already be pregnant," I told her in a low voice, knowing that Paco was probably outside the dressing room and not wanting him to overhear. "We haven't been using anything. Not once. He thought I was on the pill and I just assumed he wasn't using anything because he wanted to start our family right away. When we talked earlier I didn't bring up the fact that I might already be pregnant."

"Holy crap. What are you going to do if you are, Scarlett?"

I fell back against the chair, pushing my hair out of my face as I glared up at the ceiling. "That's the million-dollar question now, isn't it?" I released a humorless laugh. "A baby could mean giving up Ciro, because I can't get rid of it." Tears unexpectedly filled my eyes and I was helpless to hold them back. "I love him more than life, Tor. What am I going to do?"

She was up and across the luxurious little room in a heartbeat. She crouched down in front of me and we wrapped our arms around each other. I buried my face in her hair as a sob threatened to tear my body apart. "Sh, sh," she whispered, glancing at the door before lifting her eyes to mine. "First, you don't know if you are or not. How big of a chance is there?"

I scrubbed at the tears that still continued to fall. “I haven’t let myself really think about it, but if I’m honest I’d be more surprised if I wasn’t pregnant. We’ve had a lot of sex and I’m halfway through my cycle. You know how regular I am. I can count down to the hour my period will start.”

She nodded, her eyes sightless on the wall above my head as she thought about what I’d just told her. “Okay. So it’s probably way too early for you to know one way or another. Right?”

I shrugged. “Probably. I doubt an over-the-counter test would pick that up until I’m late.” At least I didn’t think it would. Which meant having to wait a few more weeks until I knew one way or another.

Victoria stood and crossed to the door. Opening it, she stuck her head out. “Anya, can you come help me with something?”

I sat up straight in the chair. “What the hell are you doing?” I whispered fiercely. I had told her because I trusted her not to tell anyone, yet she was asking the other woman to join us?

Victoria shot me a glance over her shoulder. “Anya is trustworthy and she can help you.”

“How?” I demanded, glancing at Paco’s shadow on the wall just a few feet from where my twin stood.

“I don’t know yet, but I trust her.” Anya appeared at the door and my sister stepped back to let her in, closing the door behind them.

“What’s up?” she said when she saw I was already dressed and had obviously been crying. “You getting cold feet?”

Victoria stepped closer to her and whispered something in her ear. Anya's lashes lowered, hiding her reaction from me. "What do you think?" she asked when she pulled back.

Anya grimaced but kept her voice at a low whisper when she spoke. "It probably is too early to use an at-home test. The only way to find out this early is a blood test. I know a doctor. He won't say anything to anyone, but that means losing the entourage out there. Especially if she doesn't want Ciro knowing. I'm not sure Mary will keep that kind of thing to herself. Pretty sure she would want to know if she was going to be a grandmother."

"I can't go to a doctor without Paco and Antony, and they'll tell him."

"They won't know that you're the one seeing the doctor," Victoria assured me. "I'll just pretend to be lightheaded. No one will question it."

Anya pulled her phone from her purse. "I can make it happen right now, Scarlett. It's up to you."

I bit my lip, uncertainty filling me. I had to know the truth before I married Ciro. If I waited, then found out I was pregnant and he didn't want me to keep our baby, I wasn't sure what I would do. Blinking back a fresh flood of tears, I touched a hand to my stomach. I nodded because I couldn't have spoken around the lump in my throat if I'd tried.

Anya touched something on her phone, then put it to her ear. She spoke in rapid Russian and I couldn't keep up with her but she was quickly putting the phone away. "He can do it in half an hour," she assured me.

"How long will it take before we know something?" Victoria asked, glancing at the door again.

"He can do the lab work himself and know within an hour." She glanced from me to the door. "We need to go now though, because it's going to take a little while to get there."

"Okay. I got this." Victoria turned for the door. "Give me ten minutes."

After the door closed behind her, Anya took the empty chair. I cleared my throat, forcing down the lump that was trying to suffocate me. "Thank you," I told her belatedly.

"No thanks needed," she told me with a small smile. "Victoria and I have bonded over the last few weeks, Scarlett. She's the closest thing to a friend I've ever had and I would do anything for her. Which means I would do anything for you as well. Friends help each other, right?"

I nodded, wiping away the last of the tears. My head was starting to ache from all the crying and I knew I probably looked like a hot mess. "Yes, they help each other." I glanced at the door again when there was a light tap. It hadn't been ten minutes, but Victoria was good at convincing people to do what she wanted them to. Nona was wrapped around her finger tighter than anyone else I'd ever seen.

Anya stood and let her back in, but when Victoria entered the room again she looked like she'd seen a ghost. "What is it?" I demanded as I jumped to my feet, pushing my own issues to the side at the look in her eyes. "Are you okay?"

"It's nothing. I just thought I saw Adrian outside." She clenched her jaw. "He's been trying to call me the last few days."

"Hell," Anya grumbled. "He probably followed me here. I'm sorry, Victoria."

Her smile was brittle, but she tried to put on a brave face. "It's okay. Really. Let's go out the back, though. I don't want to talk to him right now."

I opened the door and glanced at Paco, who was standing at attention, his eyes on the front of the studio that was now empty. "Tell Antony to pull the car around back," I commanded. "Volkov is out there and I don't want Victoria to have to deal with his ass right now."

He nodded. "Whatever you want, Miss Vitucci."

Paco was gone for less than half a minute. We headed to the back of the studio, bypassing the seamstress and the designer as we found the emergency door. Victoria had sent her own guards with the others, but since she was going to be with me there was no real need for the extra men. We would both probably hear it later from Papa, though.

He opened the door and glanced out before reaching for my arm. I stepped outside with him and he opened the back of the Town Car Ciro had made available for me. As I climbed in the back, Victoria and Anya got in on either side of me. Paco had barely closed the door behind my sister when we saw Adrian come around the corner of the studio.

I heard Victoria's sharp gasp at the sight of him. "Let's go," I snapped at Antony, who was behind the wheel.

Instead of doing as I told him, he just sat there, watching as Adrian came closer. I leaned forward, glaring at the man. "Let's go, Antony. My sister doesn't want to see Volkov."

"No, but he wants to see her," Antony said as he pulled the keys from the ignition.

Anya groaned. "I knew you looked familiar," she muttered and, leaning forward, punched the guard in the back of the head. "Scarlett, your man needs to find more loyal soldiers."

Fuck. I glanced at Paco, who already had his gun out. He pointed it at Antony's head, making us all sit back. "Keys, now," he roared.

Antony tossed them at the other man, then jumped out of the driver's seat as Volkov drew even closer. I glanced at the Russian, saw that his eyes were glued to my sister's face. He looked determined and pissed. I wanted to take Paco's gun and shoot him in the heart, to see if he had one and if he would actually bleed. Beside me, Victoria seemed to be in a trance as she looked back at the man. I wasn't even sure she was breathing.

Anya climbed over the seat and took Antony's place behind the wheel. Before I could even comprehend what she was doing, she snatched the gun out of Paco's hand and fired it twice at Antony, hitting him in each leg. "*Pidor*," she snarled at him in Russian as he fell to his knees beside the car. "*Idi nahui*."

The door slammed shut and she tossed the gun back at Paco, who was gaping at her in stunned amazement. “Close your damn mouth,” she told him as she switched gears and hit the gas, driving away just as her brother reached the car and tried to open Victoria’s door.

“Anya,” he bellowed after us.

Only as we drove away did Victoria snap out of her Adrian daze and realize what had happened. I was still replaying everything in my head. How Anya taken charge of the whole situation. The way she’d unflinchingly shot Antony in the legs. Anya was a badass and my new best friend.

Paco had his phone in his hand, but I reached forward and snatched it from him before he could call Ciro. “Not yet,” I told him.

“I have to tell the *capo* what happened, Miss Vitucci,” he explained.

“You can. Later.” I rolled down the window and tossed the phone out before he could take it back. I couldn’t face Ciro right then. If I saw him, if I heard his voice, I wouldn’t be able to go through with the blood test. I’d take my chances and marry him without knowing for sure. Maybe make the wrong ones that could leave us both miserable forever if I waited.

“What the fuck?” He glowered at me. “Have you lost your mind? *Capo* is going to kill someone over this.”

He was right, but I’d worry about that later. Along with a million other complications if I was pregnant.

Anya hit the brakes, making us all lurch forward. She turned to face Paco with a deadly scowl on her beautiful face. She was fast—faster than Paco could ever dream of being, because she snatched the gun from him for the second time and pointed it right at his head. "You can either go with us and do it without complaint or you can get out and walk from here. Which do you think Donati would want you to do?"

He blew out a harsh sigh. "I'll go with you." Anya lowered the gun and hit the gas again. "Wherever the hell that is."

Beside me, Victoria was watching out the back window. "Did that just happen?"

"Yes, Tor. Anya is a superhero. I think I'm a little in love with her right now."

Chapter 27

Ciro

"Two more days. Got cold feet yet?"

I didn't even spare Dante a glance as we rode through one of the more questionable parts of the city. We'd gotten a lead on where Jr might be laying low since he'd gotten back to New York, but so far we'd run into dead ends. He was a slippery sonofabitch, but I'd catch him and make sure he joined the other bottom feeders in the Hudson.

"Nope," I told him honestly. I was ready to get it over with, make Scarlett my wife and start our life together.

The talk about babies kept trying to sneak its way into my head, but I pushed it back every time. My gut twisted each time her pale face would flood my mind. Knowing she'd been hurt at first, and then so accepting when I'd told her why I didn't want kids, was like a kick to the teeth.

I hadn't realized she wanted my child until today. She'd looked so happy until I'd squashed her fantasy about our kids.

Fuck.

I should have thought about protection from the first night. Instead I'd jumped to the conclusion she was taking care of it. I hadn't let myself think about what us going unprotected for over two weeks could mean. Sweat beaded my forehead every time I thought about it, along with Scarlett's words from earlier.

You are enough for me, Ciro. Nothing else will ever make me as happy as being loved by you.

You're a good man and I love you completely.

I love you despite the things you might have done in the past. Despite what you might have to do in the future.

Our child would love you too.

Our child. Fuck. Why did those two words make my heart stop? Why was I so focused on them when she'd told me that she wouldn't push the subject? That she wouldn't ever bring it up again because I was all she wanted?

Because I wanted to believe that our child really would love me. That I could love it.

Fuck.

"So if this isn't you getting cold feet, what's up with the sweating? Are you getting sick?" He shifted closer toward the driver's window as he watched me out of the corner of his eye. "I don't want that shit, man. Keep it to yourself."

I wiped my hand across my forehead. I really was sweating bullets. I was letting this whole baby thing eat at me too damn much.

"You forget how to talk?"

I cracked my knuckles. "Leave it alone, Dante."

"Is she getting cold feet, then?" He chuckled when I felt the blood drain from my face. What if she did get cold feet? "Relax, my friend. Scarlett would never do that to you. She's loved you since she was, like, eleven."

"How do you know that?" I growled before I could stop myself.

The chuckle turned into a full-fledged laugh. "Rein it in, Ciro. You don't have anything to worry about where I'm concerned. Scarlett's like my little sister. We're close. We always have been. You know that. So don't get yourself twisted over it."

I sat back, reminding myself that I had nothing to be jealous of where Dante was concerned. He was right. She loved me, not him.

My phone went off and I pulled it out of my pocket as Dante stopped for a red light. Desi's voice filled my ear when I connected the call. "Paco's phone just went dead, boss. I got an alert when it did."

"So call Antony," I told him even as dread filled my stomach. I'd made sure that the men watching over Scarlett had new phones. They were programed to alert Desi when they were turned off, so in case something happened to one of them I would know about it immediately.

"He won't pick up. The GPS still shows that it's outside the studio where the women were supposed to be." There was hesitation in his voice, which wasn't like Desi. He normally told me everything I needed to know up front and was done with it.

"Go check it out," I told him, trying not to let the sudden bad feeling I had in my gut push out any thoughts of common sense. Scarlett would bust my balls if I overreacted and showed up at the studio where she was trying on her dress. My mother would kick my ass if I saw the dress before the wedding.

"I'm here now, *capo*."

I clenched my hands into fists. "And?"

Desi sighed, as if dreading what he was about to say. "So are the cops."

"What the fucking hell? Just spit it out, Des. Is Scarlett okay?" Dante shot me a look, not bothering to touch the gas when the light turned green.

"The women left about an hour ago. The seamstress saw everyone but the twins and Anya Volkov go out the front with the men. She didn't see Paco and the others leave, but heard the back door's buzzer go off and assumed they left that way. A few minutes later she heard two gunshots and then squealing tires. The woman called the cops and they showed up. There's two patches of blood on the pavement, *capo*."

My blood turned to ice. *Jr*. It was the first thought that ran through my head, but at the same time something didn't feel right about all of it. Jr wouldn't ambush anyone unless he had an entire army of men with him, too much of a chicken-shit to do anything alone. Anya had been with Scarlett, and I knew she was just as capable as five men when it came down to it. She could deal with a little weasel like Jr on her own with no trouble.

"Trace Scarlett's phone. Talk to the cops and find out what they know and tell them I'm on my way." The cops knew who I was. They wouldn't do anything unless I told them to.

Dante was still waiting when I hung up on Desi. The people behind us were blowing their horns, trying to make him move forward, but he just sat there, waiting. "You know where that fucking designer's studio is?" He nodded. "Then let's go. Now."

He did a U-turn then and there, cutting off three vehicles, making them have to swerve to avoid hitting us. "Allegra?" he bit out.

"She left with my mother apparently." I didn't pay attention to what he was doing as he drove through the city at triple the legal speed limit. Lifting my phone, I called Scarlett's phone but it went to voicemail after only a few rings. Hanging up without leaving a message, I called my mother next. It rang twice before she picked up.

"Hi, sweethea—"

I cut her off. "Ma, is Scarlett with you?"

"No. We haven't seen her in about half an hour. Victoria said she had a surprise for Scarlett and that they would catch up with us at dinner," my mother told me. "Is everything okay?"

"I'll call you back," I promised without telling her anything. As soon as I disconnected with her, I called Cristiano. "Have you talked to your sisters?"

"Victoria called earlier today. She was on her way to the dress appointment with Nona and Allegra."

"Fuck. Get over to that studio. Something's going on. I'll tell you more when I know something." He didn't ask questions, not that I could have given him answers. I didn't know anything.

By the time we got there the cops were gone, but Desi was behind the building. Even driving like a Formula One contender, it had still taken Dante over half an hour to get to the studio. Desi was standing beside two dark spots on the pavement. Blood. My gut twisted again, making it hard to breathe for a second. In his hand were two phones. I glanced around, looking for any sign that might tell me what was going on and where Scarlett was. Dante crouched down to examine the blood stains.

Desi lifted his head when I reached him. He offered me the second phone in his hands. "The cops found this down the alley over there."

"Antony's?"

He nodded. "Yeah. Interesting last call, though."

I pulled up the call history and found a number I didn't recognize. There was no name listed and I didn't expect there to be. We didn't assign names to anyone, ever. Pushing send, I lifted it to my ear and waited. It rang over and over again until a deep voice answered. "Figured you would call."

Some of the dread that was knotting my stomach eased at the sound of Volkov's voice. He wouldn't hurt Scarlett…would he?

"Why's that?" I asked in a neutral voice, unsure of what the Russian had to do with Scarlett being missing. I reined in the hold on my impatience, knowing that rushing this particular man would get me nowhere.

"Your man is okay. Took two to the kneecaps, though. Anya is a dead shot." He grunted and I thought I heard ice clinking against glass. "You'll probably want his head, though. He's my man too. The idiot can't do shit right anyway."

"Which man?" I bit out, trying to wrap my head around what was going on. Not Paco. I knew he would never betray me by working for anyone but me, even someone who was supposedly an ally.

"Antony." He slurred the name and I realized he was drunk. Ice clinked again. "She ran from me. No, fuck that. She didn't run. Anya stole her away. Fucking traitorous *suka*. Why would she run when she knows I love her?"

I scrubbed my hand over my face, frustrated with the whole situation and losing hold of my patience. Behind me I heard Cristiano call my name but didn't turn around. Dante said something to him, and they became quiet, watching me as I waited for Volkov to give me the information I would have paid any price for right then.

"Where is Scarlett?" I tried to keep my voice even and cold when he didn't say another word, just drank more of whatever he was numbing himself up with. I didn't pull it off, though, my voice cracking on her name.

Volkov swallowed audibly, taking another long drink. "Fuck if I know. Anya drove away before I could get Victoria out."

My patience had completely run out now. If the man had been standing in front of me I would have blown his brains on the ground. "You'd better be telling me the truth, Volkov. Because if something happens to them, it's on you." I hung up. Swallowing a curse, I turned my attention on Desi. "Did you get anything off the trace on Scarlett's phone?"

He nodded. "That's even more weird. I was able to track her movements from the last hour. She went to some clinic over in Brighton Beach for a little while, then started moving again. As far as I can tell she's on her way home."

Brighton Beach. Russian territory. Anya must have taken them there. The clinic made no sense unless one of them was sick, but there were closer urgent care and ERs between there and Brighton Beach. She was on her way home, though. My relief was so strong it nearly knocked the air out of my chest.

Turning away from the three other men, I headed for the street. I felt physically sick after the scare of losing Scarlett again. Something was going on, but I couldn't bring myself to care what it was. She was on her way home. Safe.

Nothing else mattered.

"Ciro," Cristiano called after me. "What the fuck is going on? Where are my sisters?"

I didn't answer. If I so much as opened my mouth I was going to throw up.

Scarlett

I sat on the couch with Victoria on one side of me and Anya on the other. Both were holding my cold hands. I needed their warmth after the phone call I'd just gotten.

After what had happened with Adrian and Antony, Anya had driven us to Brighton Beach where her doctor friend had been waiting. He'd taken some blood, then promised to call as soon as he had the results. We'd gotten all the way back to the apartment before he'd made the call.

I was pregnant.

"The hCG levels in your blood work show that you are either further along than you indicated, or perhaps having twins," his thickly accented voice had informed me. "As you are obviously an identical twin yourself, the chance…" After that I'd tuned him out. Victoria had taken the phone and listened to what he said, but I didn't care.

There was no way I could possibly be further along than I'd told him. Ciro had been the first man to touch me. He would be the last.

If he still wanted me.

What was I going to do? I'd promised him I wouldn't bring up children again, that it didn't matter to me if we never had them. It had been the truth, but now that I knew that Ciro's child was growing inside me, I couldn't be sad about it. I wasn't happy either. How could I be when it could mean that I might lose him?

Vaguely I heard Victoria say something to Anya, but I didn't understand their words. They were talking in Russian and my brain was too clouded to make sense of any of it. My sister shifted against me, placing her arm around me and resting her head on my shoulder. A soft throw was draped around me and a warm mug was pressed into my numb hands.

"Drink," Anya commanded, and because I'd seen what she could do when tested, I lifted the drink to my lips and took a small sip. The tea was weak and sickly sweet and I quickly lowered my hands, only to have Anya lift them back up. "You need this. Just drink."

Rather than argue with her, I drank it all in two big swallows. When I was done she set the cup on the end table beside her and tucked the throw around me a little tighter. She and Victoria were treating me like a small child, but I couldn't think of a single reason to stop them from babying me. I was just thankful that someone was there to hold me together while I slowly fell apart.

A door slamming made Victoria jump beside me and I was finally pulled out of my fog enough to turn my head and see who had come in. Seeing Ciro standing in the middle of the room, his face gray and drawn, his blue eyes like storm clouds, I was jerked completely out of my shock.

Victoria jumped to her feet. "I can explain. I got sick and—" She broke off when he shifted his eyes to her and his head slowly cocked to the side. He looked dangerous. Right then he was a predator, I his prey, and he was ready to destroy my sister if she didn't get out of his way. My twin's mouth snapped shut and she looked over at Anya. "Maybe we should go."

The other woman stood. "I'm not sorry about shooting your man. He deserved it."

Ciro just stood there, not moving so much as an eyelash until the door shut behind them. I opened my mouth, ready to tell him everything, when suddenly he was in front of me and jerking me up off the couch and into his arms. He tucked my head against his chest and my legs went instinctively around him. He was shaking so hard that he barely had time to fall onto the couch before we both ended up on the floor.

His heart was beating at a crazy rate, his breathing coming in pants that made me wonder if he was having a panic attack. I hugged him tight. "I'm sorry," I whispered. "I didn't mean to scare you."

"Just… just shut up," he muttered in a voice that shook.

I pressed my lips against his neck. "I'm sorry," I repeated.

"Baby, I'm trying not to throw up right now, so, please…shut up. Let me hold you."

I kept quiet. Tears filled my eyes, but I didn't let them fall. He was already upset enough and I didn't want to add to it when I knew this was going to get worse when I told him about the baby. Or was it babies? I hadn't paid enough attention to the doctor to remember. God, that was even worse. He didn't want one, how would he handle two?

Slowly his heart calmed down and his shaking faded into tremors that assaulted him every few minutes. Carefully, I lifted my head. His eyes were closed and his face was still gray but not quite as drawn as it had been. He looked destroyed, defeated.

Blue eyes popped open. "Where were you?"

I swallowed around the lump in my throat that I hadn't been able to completely get rid of all evening. "I went to a doctor Anya knows." His jaw tensed and I rushed on before I lost my nerve. "After what you said earlier today I had to know if I was pregnant or not. I couldn't wait for a missed period, I needed to know now in case I was." He just looked up at me and my chin started to tremble, tears filling my eyes as I prepared myself for his explosion. "I'm pregnant," I whispered and closed my eyes.

The explosion never came. He didn't start yelling. His body remained just as it had moments before. Cautiously I opened my eyes. His face had lost some of the grayness, and there was a glitter in his eyes that made my heart crack open. Was he crying?

"Ciro, I'm sorry. I didn't mean for this to happen. Please believe that." He didn't even open his mouth and panic started to burn through my body. The first tear fell onto my cheek but I didn't dare wipe it away. "I love you and I know I told you we didn't have to have a baby, but… I can't get rid of it. Please don't ask me to because I think it might kill me if you do."

I was sobbing now, uncontrollably. My fingers clenched in his shirt, desperately holding on to him even though I knew I was probably going to lose him anyway.

Rough hands cupped my face, lifting my chin until I was meeting his gaze again. A few of his own tears had spilled free. "I love you, *vita mia*. You are my life. I would never—not ever—ask you to get rid of our child. Do you understand me?"

"But you said…"

"I've said a lot of stupid things in my life, none more so than what I said this afternoon. After the things I've done, I was scared of not being able to love my child, Scarlett. It was terrifying to think about it. Some of the things I've done…" He stopped, clenched his jaw and shook his head. "It's made me hard. Emotionless at times. I've had to start turning parts of myself off, baby. I've become a monster. After a while I thought I would never get those parts back. That all I had left was just for you."

My heart broke all over again for him. "You're not a monster."

Ciro wiped away one of my tears with his thumb, a sad self-decrepitating smile on his face. "Thank you for thinking that, *vita mia*." He stroked his thumb downward until he reached the base of my throat. "I was wrong about not being able to love my own child, though. When you said you were pregnant just now, it was like I'd been hit with a lightning bolt of love." His other hand moved to caress my stomach. “This baby will never know anything but love, I swear to you.”

“Really?” I breathed, unable to completely believe what he was saying.

“Really.” He had said it like a vow, his hand settling protectively over where I could picture our baby—or babies—already securely nestled. “I love you. I love this new life we’ve created together. It’s part of you, Scarlett. How could I not love it?”

New tears blinded me as I dropped against his chest, but these were different. They were happy tears that I couldn’t hold back without imploding. A sob-filled laugh escaped me as I held on to him and he held me back. I was drunk off relief that he didn’t hate me, that he wanted and loved our baby just as much as I already did.

I felt his lips on my neck. “No matter what I do in the future, *vita mia*, no matter what I have to do to make sure you and our child are safe, I will always love you.”

“I love you, Ciro.”

Epilogue

Ciro

It was the middle of the day and I probably should have been working, but instead I was lying in the middle of the baby-proofed living room floor with my daughter trying to fall asleep on my chest. Her soft weight couldn't have held me down more if it weighed a ton. The smell of clean sweet baby that filled my nose was my new favorite scent.

Fighting sleep, she lifted her head, her blue eyes squinting before she gave me a toothless smile and drooled all over my shirt. With that smile she owned me even more so than her mother did. My heart clenched painfully, but I welcomed the discomfort. I'd never thought I could love anything or anyone as much as I did Scarlett, yet right there in my arms was one half of the proof that I could and did.

"Are you going to nap for Papa, my little Zariah?" I murmured in a soft voice that she'd always seemed fascinated with.

Her lips opened and closed, trying to talk to me, but no words came out. Instead I was treated to the slobbery raspberry she blew, making me laugh with delight. All too soon I knew she would start to talk and then walk. I dreaded those first little steps she would take, knowing they were only the beginning of her leaving me behind. Scarlett thought it was funny that I was already worried about our children growing up, but it was my new nightmare.

"Ciro, where…" Scarlett's voice trailed off as she came into the living room and spotted me on the floor with Zariah on my chest. Her brown eyes softened and my heart twisted in my chest at the love I saw shining back at me. "Well, that explains her. Now where is the boy?"

I turned my head and she followed my gaze to where Zayne was trying to belly-crawl his way toward the couch. He hadn't gotten far in the few minutes since I'd joined the twins on the floor, but there was determination on his face as he aimed for his ultimate goal. The twins were barely five months old, but Zayne was already showing signs of being just like me. I dreaded his future antics, but Scarlett was enjoying every second of our son's escapades. His sister was a mixture of both Scarlett and me, which could be explosive at times, but she knew exactly how to wrap me around her chubby little finger.

Letting out a mock huff, she marched across the room and lifted our son into her arms. Angry blue eyes glared up at her for stopping his progress, but when she kissed his chubby cheek, his arms wrapped around her neck, holding her against him like he never wanted her to let him go.

Laughing, she tickled his stomach and then carried him over to join me and Zariah on the floor. With Zayne on her lap, she gave me a smirk. “I thought you had meetings this morning with the other *capos* at Papa’s?”

“Something more important came up,” I told her. There was nothing more important that getting to snuggle with my baby girl.

Her eyes were laughing down at me, but she nodded with complete seriousness. “So I see.” She stroked her hand over our daughter’s back, getting an angry cry in response because the baby thought her mother was going to take her away from me. Scarlett rolled her eyes. “Spoiled little daddy’s girl.”

I sat up with Zariah still on my chest. Rubbing my chin against her cheek made her giggle, which filled my heart to nearly overflowing at the sweet sound. Little fingers pushed into my mouth, wanting me to nibble at them. I gave her what she wanted for a few seconds, then reluctantly handed her over to Scarlett. Leaning forward, I kissed my wife on the lips long and hard, much to my son’s annoyance.

Pulling back, I winked down at her and then got to my feet. Vito wasn’t likely to accept that I’d been held up all day by his beloved granddaughter. I had responsibilities that required my attention. As soon as I walked out that door, I wouldn’t be the loving husband and father I was right then. I’d learned to leave that part of myself right there in

Scarlett's safekeeping, knowing that as soon as I felt her lips on mine at the end of the day that I'd be whole again and turn back into the man who worshiped her and our twins. "Love you, *vita mia*."

"We love you too, Papa."

Acknowledgements

There are so many people I want to give a shout out to. First and foremost, my readers. Thank you all so much from the bottom of my heart. It's because of you that I continue to write and as long as you ask for more, that is exactly what I'll give you. Your love for every character I give you overwhelms me each and every time. LG, MC, and LJ…I can never tell you how much I appreciate you. The three of you keep me sane whether it's real life drama or writing. Thank you for being the voices of reason and showing me that killing off a major character isn't the answer when there are perfectly good secondary ones that can easily withstand a little torture here and there. Thank you, thank you, thank you to my amazing editor, Lorelei, who has been with me since The Rockers' Babies. She takes my crazy babbling and turns it into something worth reading. I can only imagine the migraines I've given her over the years. To my children, thank you for understanding that when Mommy's in the cave, she's probably lost her mind and shouldn't be approached. For accepting that even though I don't leave the house like other mommies do, that I do in fact have an actual job that requires my attention at odd hours of the day and night. And especially for loving me despite zoning out on you in the middle of normally everyday events because a new plot twist or character has entered my head. To the ever amazing Mike Browning, my husband and partner in life as well as work, thank you for helping me take my love for writing and turning it into a career. Without you, none of this would be possible. You're there when I'm losing my mind and becoming so much a part of the writing process that I act like I'm going through some crazy breakup with a person who only exists in my head. I love you more than anything. Then. Now. Forever.

Upcoming Releases by Terri Anne Browning

A Rocker Series Novella
Needing the Memories (Drake and Lana)

Tainted Knights Rocker Series
Tainted Kiss (Kale)
Tainted Butterfly (Gray)

Angel's Halo MC
Angel's Halo: Atonement (Raider)

The Vitucci Mafiosos
Book 2 (Title coming soon)

About the Author

Terri Anne Browning is the USA TODAY bestselling author of The Rocker...Series. She started writing her own novellas at the age of sixteen, forcing her sister to be her one woman fan club. Now she has a few more readers and a lot more passion for writing. Being dyslexic, she never thought a career in writing would be possible, yet she has been on bestselling lists multiple times since 2013. Reese: A Safe Haven Novella was her first Indie published book. The Rocker Who Holds Me changed the tables and kicked off The Rocker... series featuring the sinfully delicious members of Demon's Wings. The Rocker... Series has since expanded to OtherWorld with Axton Cage and his band members. Other books by Terri Anne include the Angel's Halo MC Series as well as The Lucy & Harris Novella Series. Terri Anne lives in Virginia with her husband, their three demons---err, children--and a loveable Olde English Bulldog named Link.

Terri Anne's Reading Order:

The Rocker...Series
The Rocker Who Holds Me
The Rocker Who Savors Me
The Rocker Who Needs Me
The Rocker Who Loves Me
The Rocker Who Holds Her
The Rockers' Babies

The Rocker Who Wants Me
The Rocker Who Cherishes Me
The Rocker Who Shatters Me
The Rocker Who Hates Me
The Rocker Who Betrays Me
Forever Rockers

Angel's Halo MC Series
Angel's Halo
Angel's Halo: Entangled
Angel's Halo: Guardian Angel
Angel's Halo: Reclaimed

The Lucy & Harris Novella Series
Catching Lucy
Craving Lucy
Rocking Kin
Un-Shattering Lucy

CPSIA information can be obtained
at www.ICGtesting.com
Printed in the USA
FSHW021948180421
80599FS